ESTROG

D0034846

PART TWO

BOOK OF THE STARS

THE
*M*YSTERY
OF
*L*ORD *S*HA

Erik L'Homme

SCHOLASTIC INC.
New York   Toronto   London   Auckland   Sydney
Mexico City   New Delhi   Hong Kong   Buenos Aires

First published in the United Kingdom in 2004 by The Chicken House, 2 Palmer Street, Frome, Somerset BA11 1DS.
Email: chickenhouse@doublecluck.com

ISBN 0-439-65073-9

12 11 10 9 8 7 6 5 4 3 2 1   6 7 8 9 10 11/0

Printed in the U.S.   40

First Scholastic paperback edition, February 2006

TO...
(she knows who she is),
without whom Book of the Stars
would not be what it is.

To the two little foxes,
for lots of reasons.

To Remy, Claire and Raffeal,
who were the first to come to the signing table where I waited shyly...
— E L H

Thanks to Chloe Schwartz
and Sue Rose.
— R S

CONTENTS

THE STORY SO FAR

Thirteen-year-old Robin Penmarch lives on The Lost Isle, a remote land between The Real World and The Uncertain World, where there are computers and cinemas but you're also likely to bump into knights in armor and sorcerers with amazing powers.

When Master Quadehar, the most famous Sorcerer of the Guild, discovers that Robin has a special gift for magic, the boy's destiny is sealed.

While still at school, Robin becomes an apprentice sorcerer, learning the art of magic and the Graphems from his new master. These Graphems, the keys to sorcery, were recorded in the *Book of the Stars*. Unfortunately, this precious work was stolen from the Guild many years ago, and nobody knows its present whereabouts.

One day, monsters from the dark and dangerous Uncertain World suddenly appear on The Lost Isle. Acting on the orders of The Shadow, an evil power, they kidnap Agatha Balangru, the school bully, in front of Robin's eyes. But it is a case of mistaken identity. When Robin, who has been taken to the foreboding Monastery of Gifdu for safety, finds out that The Shadow is actually after *him*, he decides to escape from his prison and go to The Uncertain World to free Agatha. He needs all his rudimentary magic to assist him.

Robin takes his lifelong friends — Amber, Godfrey, Romaric, and Coral — with him on this risky adventure. But he doesn't get the spell quite right and the five friends are separated. They experience a series of extraordinary adventures and narrow escapes in a world inhabited by weird and wonderful creatures.

While Amber meets a female magician with green eyes who puts a spell on her to make her lose her memory of their encounter, Robin meets Kyle, a boy who lives in the perilous Ravenous Desert.

When he finally reaches the town of Yadigar, the friends' meeting place, Robin is taken prisoner. You can imagine his surprise when he finds his friends in captivity and, ultimately, Agatha Balangru — all of them imprisoned by the evil Commander Thunku, who rules over the town with an iron fist.

Thanks to Master Quadehar's intervention and Robin's magic, the six young people manage to escape.

They all return to The Lost Isle safe and sound, but there are still a lot of unanswered questions. Who is behind The Shadow, and why is he so keen to get his hands on Robin? Who is the mysterious Lord Sha that Agatha has heard tales about in Yadigar and is rumored to be looking for his long-lost son? What secret surrounds the apprentice sorcerer, and what will be his destiny?

1

BROMOTUL CASTLE

Robin hurried along the path, listening out for the sound of pounding hooves. He didn't want to get in the way of the Knights of the Wind astride their powerful chargers. It was early autumn, and the heather on Korrigans heath was already taking on a melancholy hue, heralding a harsh winter.

Robin was on his way to Bromotul Castle, the fortress training school of the Brotherhood. He was hurrying not because he was afraid of the Korrigans' tricks — for they never went near the path — but because he had some exciting news and he was impatient to share it with Romaric.

He became so absorbed in his thoughts that he didn't see two knights in turquoise armor galloping full tilt toward him. He dived into the bushes just in time to avoid being crushed under the chargers' hooves. The Knights of the Wind cursed under their breath and brought their steeds to a halt in a cloud of dust.

"Whoa there! Are you all right, son?"

"I'm fine, I'm fine," replied Robin, blushing as he extricated himself from the bush that had cushioned his fall.

The horses snorted. Luckily for Robin, the knights had them on a tight rein. Robin flicked back the lock of chestnut hair that tumbled onto his forehead and limped over to the men on horseback. He looked up at them with his startling green eyes.

"It's my fault," he apologized, trying to smile. "I was daydreaming. I didn't hear you coming."

"The main thing is that you aren't hurt," replied one of the knights.

"I bet you're a new squire on your way to Bromotul," said the other knight, who was as tall and slim as his companion was dark and stocky.

"Uh . . . no," said Robin, flushing deep crimson.

The knight had just reminded him that six months earlier, his wildest and dearest wish had been to belong to the Brotherhood of the Knights of the Wind.

"Come on, Ambor," said the knight who had spoken first. "Can't you see that the lad is carrying the canvas bag of an apprentice sorcerer?"

"Oh yes, of course!" exclaimed Ambor. "But in that case, Bertolen . . ."

Bertolen and Ambor exchanged a look, and then stared at Robin with curiosity.

"You wouldn't happen to be Robin Penmarch, would you? The boy who went to The Uncertain World and fought The Shadow's forces?"

Robin hesitated, then nodded. After his exploits last summer, his name had become famous throughout The Lost Isle and he couldn't get used to it.

The knights were impressed.

"We are honored to meet you, Robin!" exclaimed Bertolen.

"No, no, really, the honor is mine," stammered Robin, embarrassed by so much enthusiasm and admiration.

"And what brings you to the heath, Robin?" asked Ambor.

"My cousin! He's a squire at Bromotul. And today's visiting day."

"That's true," confirmed Bertolen. "But the sun is already high in the sky and you've got a good two-hour walk ahead of you. You won't have much time with your cousin."

"I know," Robin sighed. "But I had a math test this morning, and I couldn't skip school. After Dashtikazar, I managed to get a lift on a cart but it was only going a few miles."

"We know what it's like," sympathized Bertolen, winking at Ambor. "You're right, math is important, but not important enough to miss visiting day at Bromotul. Come on, jump up behind me!"

It took a few moments for Robin to grasp that the knights were offering him a ride. But he didn't waste another second and, with a huge grin, clambered up behind Bertolen.

"Awesome!" exclaimed Robin.

"Now hold on tight," warned the knight. "I don't want you landing in the bushes again!"

"Neither do I," said Robin.

Ambor and Bertolen guffawed and gave rein to the horses as they set off at a fast gallop. Robin clung to Bertolen's sword belt for all he was worth, relishing the thrill of speed. In no time at all, the massive silhouette of Bromotul Castle loomed up ahead.

Bromotul was the birthplace of the Brotherhood of Knights, the warrior order dedicated to defending The Lost Isle and protecting its inhabitants. Nowadays, the Brotherhood had a more modern and comfortable castle in the heart of the city of Dashtikazar (the capital of The Lost Isle), as well as owning several forts occupied by little garrisons in different parts of The Lost Isle. Bromotul Castle had been converted into a training school where the squires — boys selected for their promise and resolve — underwent the harsh training of a knight.

The school consisted of a huge square freestone building overlooking a dirt courtyard protected by high walls, where the students did their horsemanship exercises.

The ground floor was entirely taken up by the stables, while the cellar housed a well and the storeroom. The second floor was home to the fencing hall, gymnasium, library, and study hall.

On the third floor were the kitchen, refectory, shower rooms, and dormitories, while the weapons and equipment were kept on the top floor. There was a rather spartan feel to the whole place.

On one side, the gray walls of the fortress dominated the clifftop overlooking the sea, while on the other, they looked out over the grassy expanse of moorland. The Brotherhood bore the name of the wind which constantly battered this desolate region of The Lost Isle — a wind as wild and rugged as the knights who trained there.

Romaric was sweating and gasping for breath as he cut and thrust at the solid oak post in a corner of the courtyard, under the critical eye of the sergeant instructing him. The sword he wielded with both hands was heavy, and his shoulders ached. Sweat ran down his bare chest, and his fair hair, which he would soon have to cut short when he became a knight, was dripping wet.

"You can stop and have a rest, squire," said the instructor.

"I'm not tired," fibbed Romaric.

"Perhaps not, but others are waiting for their turn. Don't forget to clean and oil your sword before getting changed."

Romaric's place was taken by a sturdy boy who immediately struck the oak post, sending splinters of wood flying. Romaric walked over to a bench where he had left his things and sat down, panting. It was lucky the instructor had ordered him to stop. Another five minutes and he would have collapsed in a heap! He laid his sword across his knees and sighed.

He had been so thrilled when the Commander of the Brotherhood had come in person to see his parents and offer him a place at Bromotul, despite his being six months younger than the usual admission age. His father had been tremendously proud, and Uncle Urian had even sent a message to congratulate him. Romaric's dream was coming true at last! But at the time, he hadn't imagined it would be so tough.

It wasn't so much the training that he was finding difficult as the attitude of the other squires toward him. They thought he'd been given a place at Bromotul because of his exploits in The Uncertain World, rather than on merit. And even though sometimes Romaric couldn't help wondering the same thing, he worked hard to show he was equal to the task. He tried to be a good comrade-in-arms and was always prepared to go that extra mile to prove that he owed his place at the fortress training school solely to his talents.

But he was overstretching himself physically, and he felt very lonely. And to make matters worse, the village of Bounic, where his parents lived, was at the other end of the island, so he didn't receive many visits. Admittedly, Uncle Urian had already come three times, but he spent more time chatting with the elderly instructors, former knights like himself, than talking to his nephew.

The squires followed the normal school curriculum at Bromotul on top of their training. But unlike an apprentice sorcerer who was free the minute he left his master, Romaric had no time off except during the holidays. That was a real loss for the young squire.

Romaric thought of Robin, who was probably gathering plants or discussing Graphems with Master Quadehar. Then he pictured his other friends, Godfrey, Amber, and Coral. Coral . . . he would never have dreamed that anyone as squeamish as Coral could have saved his life! Smiling to himself, he relived the incident in The Uncertain World when he had swum for his life to get away from the man-eating Gommons and then the stinging jellyfish. Exhausted, he had been convinced his last hour had come. And suddenly, Coral had appeared out of nowhere to help him reach the rafts of the People of the Sea.

Romaric shuddered and tightened his grip on his sword, which still felt too big for him. He would never run away again. Soon, he would be a knight and would be able to face any danger! He gazed determinedly at the blue steel blade. This sword, which had been presented to him at the squires' initiation ceremony and would be his for all his life, represented his greatest dream: to fight the Orks and take revenge on the Gommons single-handedly! But if he lost heart after one month of training, how would he ever achieve his ambition?

He picked up a felt cloth and concentrated on carefully cleaning his weapon.

The sound of boots broke into his thoughts. The knight in charge of keeping watch over the castle was walking toward him.

"Squire!" he bawled. "You have a visitor."

Romaric frowned. Who on earth could it be? Certainly not Uncle Urian — he never announced himself at the gate but wandered around Bromotul as if he were at home in Penmarch Castle! Intrigued, Romaric replaced his sword in its sheath, took a shirt from his bag, and slipped it on as he hurried toward the entrance gate that opened onto the heath.

2

A WELCOME VISIT

Romaric recognized a familiar figure standing at the entrance, flanked by two knights in armor. His heart leaped for joy and he raced ahead of the guard to meet his visitor.

"Robin! I don't believe it!" he whooped.

"Romaric!"

The cousins hugged each other under the amused gaze of Ambor and Bertolen.

"I should have made the connection," said Bertolen to his companion. "This squire is also named Penmarch — he could only be related to Robin."

"And Urian Penmarch, the old boy with a loud voice who goes around thumping everyone on the shoulder, is he a relative, too?" asked Ambor.

"He's our uncle," chorused Robin and Romaric, both making a face.

"He was a valiant knight in his time," broke in the guard. "Nowadays, it's true, he's a bit . . ."

"A bit of an old bore?" suggested Romaric.

The guard frowned as Ambor and Bertolen roared with laughter.

"Excuse me, Sirs," Robin politely interrupted, "but I don't have much time and Romaric and I have so much to talk about . . ."

"We're going back to Dashtikazar this evening," said Bertolen. "We'll be leaving in two hours. If you want a ride . . ."

"Thank you, that's great. I'll meet you here in a couple of hours."

"Come on, Robin!" said Romaric impatiently. "I'll show you around my new school!"

He took his cousin's arm and steered him over to the bench where he had left his things.

"Wow!" exclaimed Robin, catching sight of the sword in its sheath as Romaric picked it up and slung it over his shoulder, together with his bag. "Is that what you were telling me about in your letters? It's a lot more impressive than an apprentice's bag!"

"Yes, but it's not much use if you don't know how to wield it," the squire said with a sigh.

"Come on, you've only been training for a month," Robin said encouragingly. "When I'd only been an apprentice for a month, I couldn't remember the names of the herbs and I had no idea what ley lines were."

"Yes, you're right," admitted Romaric. "But tell me, how did you persuade the two most illustrious knights of the Brotherhood to take you under their wing?"

"Oh!" replied Robin with a wink. "That's the price of fame. I think they got a kick out of rescuing *me*."

"I see . . . except that it was fame that brought me here, too, but I have to keep proving myself," complained Romaric.

"I can't help it, it's because I look so weedy!" teased Robin. "People want to protect me! Whereas with a great strapping lad like you, they want to challenge you and test your skill."

"Well, let anybody who wants to fight me step forward," laughed Romaric, punching the air. "I'm ready for them!"

They rose and went over to the stables. Romaric showed Robin the horses the squires rode during training exercises, then he led him over to the stalls of the powerful chargers that belonged to the knights.

"We are given our sword at the start of our training and our horse at the end," he explained. "If we don't give up beforehand! If that happens, we lose everything."

"I have faith in you," said Robin, stroking the muzzle of a mare named Tornado. "I know you'll make an outstanding knight."

Romaric's face lit up.

"Did you ask the Graphems?" he asked. "Did they show you what my future would be?"

"No, but you've thumped me often enough for me to know that you were born to be a fighter!"

"Stupid!" exclaimed Romaric, pretending to hit him.

"You see? What was I saying?"

Romaric fought an urge to push his cousin over into a pile of straw. Then the two boys burst out laughing and left the stables.

They made their way to the squires' dormitory where each boy had a bed and a big chest in which to keep his personal belongings. Romaric put his sword away carefully.

Next, Romaric showed Robin the library, which was practically empty. Robin studied the shelves with interest.

"Most of the books here are military manuals and works on the art of war," Romaric said in an apologetic tone.

"Did you think I was expecting to find books on botany in a school for knights?" teased Robin. "Drop it, Romaric. You're a squire and you're training to fight, and I'm an apprentice and I'm learning magic. The Lost Isle needs both knights and sorcerers, just as it needs electricians and bakers. Nobody forces us to be anything, it's our choice, and we have to take responsibility for that choice."

Romaric gaped at his cousin in amazement. How he'd changed in just a few months. In the past, Robin had always gone to him when he needed reassurance, but now the tables had turned.

They sat in the leather armchairs used by generations of squires around a coffee table strewn with magazines on fencing and horsemanship.

"Have you heard from the others?" asked Romaric.

"Amber writes to me."

"I knew it!" said his cousin with a wink. "I think she's taken a liking to you since our trip to The Uncertain World!"

"Huh! So you're not interested in asking what she has to say, or who she talks about in her letters . . . like Coral, for example?"

"Touché!" admitted Romaric, good-naturedly. "So, what does she have to say for herself?"

"First of all, she remembered my birthday, unlike some people!"

"OK, OK," said Romaric defensively. "I promise, next year I won't forget. It's unbelievable, you turned thirteen at the equinox and you're already as bad-tempered as Uncle Urian! Now tell me what Amber says about the others in her letters."

"Well, she and Coral are both back at school in Krakal. Things are quiet there and they can't wait for the Samain holidays. By the way," he suddenly remembered, "I've got some exciting news. . . ."

"Are we still on for Samain?" Romaric interrupted him, elated at the prospect of the vacation.

"Yes . . . Amber and Coral's father has agreed to lend us his apartment in Dashtikazar. We'll have ringside seats for the festivities!"

"Great! Did Amber say anything else?"

"That she's been having weird dreams since her return from The Uncertain World."

"Weird dreams?"

"She dreams of a green-eyed woman, a stranger, and of a forest where she's never set foot in her life, as well as strange imaginary creatures."

"Yeah, right . . ." said Romaric, dubiously. "I bet she's just making it up."

"I don't know. That's not like her . . . besides, she's sick. She's been in bed for three days! You should write to her, I'm sure she'd like that."

"Three days stuck in bed. Poor thing! I bet she's in a rotten mood. But you're right. I'll drop her a line."

"That's enough about the girls," said Robin, suddenly changing the subject. "Now, listen to me. I've got something amazing to tell you!"

"Yes, yes, I know. . . ."

"You know?" gulped Robin, taken aback.

"Yes, I had a message from Godfrey. He got into the Academy of Music! He's even starting right away."

"He wrote to me, too," said Robin with a sigh of relief. *That* wasn't his big news.

His cousin didn't know anything after all; he was going to give him the surprise of his life! "That's great," he went on, "but that's not the amazing piece of news. . . ."

"Really? So what is it then?"

Just then, a noisy group of squires barged into the library, putting an end to their conversation. From their aggressive swagger, Robin guessed they were not there to study.

3

DIRTY TRICKS

One of the squires came straight up to Romaric, evidently very sure of himself.

"Hey, you!" he yelled. "Geoffrey's waiting for you in the arms room. You'd better get over there fast, unless of course you're too scared!"

His four companions snickered. They stood by the door with their arms folded like bodyguards, glaring theatrically. Robin stared at his cousin in shock.

Romaric sighed and got to his feet. "I told you that I don't have the same reputation here as you do!"

He looked his fellow squires up and down and, pointing to Robin, added with the same aggressive tone, "He'll be my second."

The boy who had challenged him accepted with a nod. Then they hustled Romaric and Robin in the direction of the arms room. Robin whispered to his cousin, "Are they challenging you to a duel?"

"Yes," Romaric whispered back. "And with the meanest thug on the planet."

"Isn't that going kind of far?"

"All right. The meanest brute Bromotul has ever seen!"

They entered the room which doubled as Bromotul's gym and fencing hall. In the center stood a tall boy with fair hair like Romaric, but older than him. He wore an ugly expression and he had a nervous twitch. Beneath his shirt, you could see his impressive muscles bulging. He was holding two big sticks.

"You're going to prove to us once and for all that you're here on merit," he snarled at Romaric, and tossed him one of the sticks.

Romaric caught the weapon in midair and adopted a fighting stance, like his opponent. "You're going to regret this, Geoffrey!" growled Romaric in reply.

Robin and the four squires moved a safe distance away. The duelists eyed each other carefully and then slowly began skirting around each other. Geoffrey lunged first. Romaric parried and counterattacked. His opponent did likewise. Romaric backed away. There were beads of sweat on his forehead.

Robin realized his cousin was not going to have an easy time of it. Mentally, he egged him on.

Suddenly, Geoffrey made a thrust and caught Romaric hard in the stomach. Winded, Romaric bent double and retreated a few steps, gasping desperately for air. His opponent, certain of victory, calmly advanced, brandishing his stick above his head, ready to finish him off. But Romaric, seizing his moment, flung himself to the ground and struck out at Geoffrey with a well-aimed kick, simultaneously bringing his stick crashing down on his attacker. Geoffrey groaned, dropped his weapon, and rolled on the floor.

Romaric got to his feet and grinned at Robin in relief. His opponent was well and truly out of action. But just at that moment, he caught sight of the other squires. They had each picked up a stick and were advancing menacingly towards him. Things were beginning to turn nasty.

The situation seemed hopeless to Robin, and he decided it was time to intervene. Besides, the squires had just proved how cowardly they were, and Robin didn't see why he should have any qualms about interfering in a contest that was so clearly one-sided. Only he had to be discreet, for it was strictly forbidden to use magic within the Brotherhood. Quadehar, his master, was forever telling him that sorcerers and knights worked together, but in very different ways. Each kept to their own specific field.

His mind was racing. What could he do? Romaric had already fended off an attack and was retreating under a volley of renewed blows.

Suddenly, a smile lit up the apprentice's face: That was it! He closed his eyes and visualized all the Graphems. He called up Ingwaz, opened his eyes again and murmured, "Ingwaz . . . Ingwaz . . . Ingwaz . . . Ingwaz . . ."

The "freezing" Graphem had to be called once for each person in order to immobilize them all. Last summer, when the Orks had attacked near Penmarch, he had forgotten that rule, and had almost paid dearly for it. But now, Robin was perfectly in control of his Graphems.

As Ingwaz hadn't been shouted loudly, but murmured gently, the squires' legs grew gradually heavier. Romaric soon noticed that his opponents were growing less agile and that their movements were becoming hampered. He seized the opportunity and leaped at one of them, knocking the stick out of his hands and hitting him on the side; the squire yelped and crumpled to the floor. Romaric easily parried a slow lumbering attack from a second squire and sent him somersaulting over his shoulder. He brought down a third with a punch in the stomach, then finished off the last one with a reverse kick that caught him in the chest. He went over to his cousin and said with a grin, "OK, so what did you do to make them so slow all of a sudden?"

"What did I do?" echoed Robin, laughing. "Nothing at all. Honestly! Looks like you gave them a real thrashing!"

"Yeah, even if you did help me!"

"Oh, I didn't do much . . . but believe me, this'll do wonders for your reputation. No one will pick on you again!"

"Unless this makes them *all* want to fight me now," sighed Romaric, dragging Robin out of the gym. "Let's not hang around. Not that I'm afraid of these idiots, but if a knight shows up and finds out magic is being used at Bromotul, I'll be in big trouble."

"Nobody will ever find out," Robin reassured him. "The effect of my Graphem will wear off in a few minutes. In any case, it's time I went to meet Ambor and Bertolen now."

They took the stairs four at a time down the majestic stone staircase that led to the main entrance.

"By the way, Robin," Romaric said suddenly as they reached the courtyard. "What was that amazing piece of news you had to tell me?"

"News, what news?" asked Robin. "Oh yes," he went on, trying to sound cool, "I simply wanted to tell you that the Sorcerers of the Guild have sifted through all the information we brought back from The Uncertain World, and now they're planning an attack on The Shadow. But keep it to yourself," he warned, running over to join Ambor and Bertolen, who were waiting for him by the gate. "It's all very hush-hush!"

Robin clambered up behind Bertolen. He waved good-bye to Romaric, who stood gaping in the middle of the courtyard, staggered by the extraordinary news. Then, as the horses galloped away, he vanished in a cloud of dust.

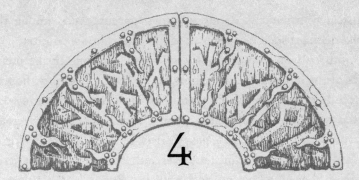

4

BIRDSONG

For a good two hours, Godfrey had been sitting in the corridors of the Academy of Music, waiting for his name to be called. He had laid his zither on a seat and was pacing up and down the flagstone floor of the entrance hall, his hands clasped behind his back. He was surprised by this poor timekeeping on the part of the tutors who would hopefully be teaching *him* to play in time — if he made it through the final interview.

Godfrey had immediately fallen in love with the long buildings of the Academy, which stood on the fringes of the Forest of Tantreval. Birdsong filled the air, vying with the sound of students practicing their scales. Three days a week, the pupils — boarders or half-boarders — received the best education for promising young musicians available on The Lost Isle.

In fact, music was of great importance throughout the land. Each village had its own orchestra, and every day a dance was held somewhere. The people of The Lost Isle loved dancing and listening to the best flautists and zither players competing in musical tournaments. Godfrey's own parents were among the most distinguished and renowned musicians in the country.

Godfrey was Romaric's closest friend, and one of the members of the gang. Tall and gangly and a little too skinny, he had carefully combed black hair and shining deep brown eyes. He had a wonderfully laid-back nature, which made him a good person to have around in times of crisis. In The Uncertain World, he had escaped from a sinister tower and, later, befriended a fierce warrior thanks to his musical abilities. But it was his performance on the zither at Uncle Urian's birthday party at Penmarch Castle that had brought him to the attention of the Academy, and so he had been invited to take the entrance exam.

"Godfrey Grum!"

Godfrey wheeled around and saw a primly dressed woman in her fifties. She asked him to follow her, and he picked up his instrument and obeyed. They entered a room with whitewashed walls and light flooding in from huge windows. Behind a table, two men and another woman sat watching him closely. The woman closed the door behind him.

"Put down your zither and stretch your arms out in front of you, palms flat," she said.

A little taken aback, Godfrey did as he was asked. The woman examined his fingers, then gave a satisfied nod.

"He's not trembling," she stated. "He doesn't seem to suffer from nerves."

Godfrey immediately understood why he had been kept waiting in the corridor. But he didn't have time to reflect on the devious methods used by the Academy's selection committee, because a member of the panel was speaking to him.

"Pick up your zither and play us 'The Ballad of Yore.'"

Godfrey did as he was told and tried his hardest to pour all his feelings into playing the ancient tune. When he had finished, the examiner sat down at the piano and played a fairly complex melody. "Now sing what you have just heard."

Godfrey sang, without omitting a single note. Next, he was given a sheet of paper and a pencil.

"Transcribe what you hear me play," the pianist instructed.

His tongue poking out, the young musician concentrated on this music dictation. His head was beginning to swim.

"Take this instrument and compose a tune of your choice based on the theme I'm about to play," continued the examiner.

She held out a flute, and played a short melody on the piano. Godfrey raised the flute to his lips and closed his eyes.

There was absolute silence in the vast room. Godfrey could feel sweat trickling down his back. His mind went utterly blank, and he froze. He was so close to his heart's desire, this was ridiculous!

He was on the point of giving up when, suddenly, he heard two birds twittering as they flew off from one of the window ledges. Their chatter inspired him, and Godfrey launched into an introductory trill. Then he interpreted the furious birdsong he had heard, working it into the musical theme the examiner had given him.

When he opened his eyes again, he saw that the four teachers no longer wore severe expressions, but were smiling at him.

"Register at the office on Monday morning and don't forget your zither. Classes will start in the afternoon."

"You mean . . ." stammered Godfrey, who hadn't dreamed

for one moment that his future would be decided so quickly, "you mean I've been accepted into the Academy?"

"Each year we take twenty new students," confirmed the woman who had tested him. "And you'll be one of them."

Godfrey said good-bye and left the room in a daze. He flopped down onto a seat in the corridor, and tried to collect his thoughts. He could already imagine the triumphant reception he'd be given by his parents, but the first thing he was going to do was send messages by carrier pigeon to Romaric, Robin, Amber, and Coral, to tell them his good news.

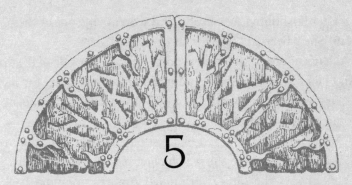

5

SECRETS

Amber flung her tennis racket onto her bed and removed her shoes, hurling them into a corner of the bedroom. Then, wiping her face on her T-shirt, she headed for the bathroom. The tennis coach had worked them hard, and from the minute she'd walked off the court all she could think about was taking a long shower. She rattled the door handle. Someone else was in the bathroom and had locked the door.

"Coral!" she yelled. "Don't tell me you're still in the tub!"

"I'll be out in a minute," replied a voice muffled by the sound of splashing.

Amber sighed. Her sister had already been in the bathroom when she'd left for her tennis lesson. Amber and Coral were twins. Amber, with her short, dark hair was strong-willed and outspoken, sporty and tough. Coral, on the other hand, with her long hair, love of clothes, and sea-blue eyes, looked as though she'd stepped straight out of a fashion magazine.

"Mom!" shouted Amber. "Coral won't come out of the bath-room! She's been in there for three hours!"

"That's not true!" protested Coral on the other side of the door. "And I'll only be another five minutes! I just need to dry my hair."

"Dry your hair!" wailed Amber. "But that'll take an hour! Mom . . . do something!"

"Now, now, girls, calm down," shouted up their mother from the sitting room where she was having tea with two friends.

"It's always the same," grumbled Amber, stomping back to her room after giving the bathroom door a thump. "Princess has her bath and everybody else has to wait until she feels like coming out!"

As she passed her sister's room, Amber hesitated, then paused. Had Coral forgotten to lock the door? She turned the handle; the door opened.

Amber slipped inside. Now was her chance to find out what Coral had been so busy scribbling about for hours on end in the notebook she called "My Diary." Amber had glimpsed the cover one day when Coral hadn't been quick enough to hide it. "My Diary" — could it get more obvious?

The bed with its pink duvet was unmade. There was no sign of the notebook on the desk, which served mainly as a dressing table. But one of the drawers was open.

Amber went over to it and spotted the precious diary. She picked it up and leafed through it, read a sentence or two, and then another, at random. It was all about Romaric! Amber turned the pages excitedly — this was going to be interesting! She was preparing to settle down and read it, when she heard the bathroom door being unlocked.

"Just my luck," she moaned. "It usually takes her ages to do her hair."

Amber rushed out and dived into her own room. She lay down on her bed and grabbed a magazine, which she pretended to read. A few seconds later, there was a knock on her door.

"Who is it?"

"Coral!"

"Come in."

Coral poked her head around the door.

"The bathroom's free now. I was as quick as I could be. I didn't think you'd be back from tennis so soon."

"Don't worry about it. Thanks."

Amber heard her sister go into her room and lock the door. She lay there for a moment thinking about Coral's little secret. She was consumed with curiosity. Why did she find it so hard to cope with the idea of her sister having a secret? Coral had started writing a diary on their return from The Uncertain World and, since then, she had confided a lot less in her twin sister. Amber's head hurt . . . she rolled over and massaged her temples.

She had been sick for three days, and although today she'd felt well enough to play tennis, she still had a bit of a headache. The doctor had diagnosed a bad cold, had prescribed lots of medicine, and left her alone to her exhaustion. Without being able to explain why, she was convinced that her headaches were connected to the disturbing dreams she'd been having recently. She'd never been ill for so long before! Before what . . . ? Before her visit to The Uncertain World, come to think of it. . . .

Amber suddenly felt gloomy. She needed something to cheer her up. She opened the drawer of her bedside table and took out three sheets of paper, crumpled from having been read and reread so many times. She started to read the first page:

Dear Amber,

I saw Robin yesterday. He came to visit me at Bromotul. He told me you were sick. That's weird, because it's hard to imagine you sick! Anyway, I hope you get better soon, and that you won't let us down for the Samain holidays! I can't wait till we're all together again. Hey, have I told you about my training? . . .

Amber smiled. She could see herself as a squire if the Brotherhood were less fuddy-duddy and old-fashioned about who it admitted.

She thought about her sister's diary and regretted not having been able to find out more about her little crush on Romaric . . . She put his letter away, grabbed a second sheet, and skimmed through Godfrey's writing:

. . . a real triumph! So here I am, a student at the Tantreval Academy of Music! Don't be jealous. One day, you'll find out where your talents lie. Robin told me you're in bed with a raging temperature — that's no joke. We're all dying for the Samain holidays. So get better right away! . . .

What was wrong with them all? Didn't they realize she was just as impatient as they were to be together again in Dashtikazar for the Samain holidays next month? Anyway, their letters had been a great comfort while she'd been lying around, moping in bed.

She picked up the last sheet, the letter from Robin, which was the most creased of all . . .

. . . in Dashtikazar, for Samain.
Love
Robin

Love! She had read and reread that phrase a hundred times. She knew it didn't mean much — you said "love" to your sister, your parents, and your grandparents. But anyway, it was something.

She heard steps in the corridor. She gave Robin's letter a quick kiss, then put the three letters away in the drawer, jumped off the bed, and hurried into the bathroom before Coral decided to go back in there.

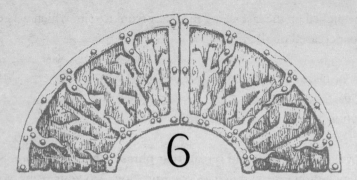

6

A RATHER SPECIAL
GEOGRAPHY LESSON

"Robin!"

Robin looked up from his textbook and gazed at the bald man with thick spectacles whose open shirt revealed a scrawny torso. He had been their history and geography teacher for the last couple of years.

"Yes, Sir?"

"Why don't you share with the class what you saw on your travels in The Uncertain World?"

Robin sighed.

Since his extraordinary adventure the summer before, his life had changed a great deal. First of all, he'd moved up to the third year at school and had had to get used to a whole set of new subjects, like the institutions of The Lost Isle, geometry, and athletics. Then, Robin's new-found fame had suddenly made him very popular with the other boys and girls at school and brought him unwanted attention from his teachers, especially the history and geography master. Otherwise, school might almost have been fun!

Robin felt the teacher's insistent gaze and the hopeful eyes of the whole class upon him. His classmates were only too delighted to deviate from the lesson and spend the rest of the time listening to him. There was a general murmur of approval as he began.

"As you know, The Uncertain World is one of the three Worlds."

"What are the other two Worlds, Camilla?" the teacher snapped at a student who was chatting at the back of the classroom.

"Er . . . The Real World and The Lost Isle?" she replied.

"Correct. And stop talking, please! Go on, Robin."

"You reach it via one of the two Doors located on a hillside outside Dashtikazar. . . ."

"Cedric, can anyone go through these Doors?" the teacher asked a boy who was looking out of the window, daydreaming.

"Sorry? I didn't hear the question, Sir."

"For goodness' sake!" the teacher snorted. "Why aren't you listening? Robin's experience is unique. You should make the most of the chance to hear about it!"

"So," Robin went on patiently, "only the sorcerers can use these Doors. The one to The Uncertain World leads to vast, wild lands, and the people who live there are pretty tough. They don't really have much choice — they have to rub shoulders with monsters like Orks and Gommons, as well as cruel men such as

Commander Thunku, who rules the city of Yadigar. This brute has an army of thugs who are only good for pillaging and war. Alongside more or less ordinary people, you find strange tribes, the Men of the Sands, for example, who live in the middle of the Ravenous Desert — which is alive and devours anything that's not stone! The People of the Sea live on rafts on the Infested Sea which is swarming with poisonous jellyfish. . . ."

As he told his tales of The Uncertain World, Robin felt a mounting excitement. Now the whole class was enthralled, and the teacher wore a proud smile.

". . . the Little Men of Virdu are the size of children, and they mine precious stones for a living; they're the bankers of The Uncertain World. They wear very comfortable cloaks . . ." Robin paused for a moment, smiling to himelf.

"There are also merchants, like here, but they have to hire mercenaries to protect their caravans from bandits. The biggest city is called Ferghana, and it's linked to its twin town of Yadigar by a stone road. In the middle of the country is a town called Yenibohor, which is occupied by evil priests. Everyone's afraid of them."

Standing at the blackboard holding a piece of chalk, the teacher drew a map of The Uncertain World, based on Robin's description.

"Surrounding Ferghana is the Sea of Great Winds, and in the far north, above the Middle Island," he added, drawing in the air to help his teacher, "are the steppes of the Uncertain North. They are inhabited by nomadic warriors. To the east, there's the Purple Forest — it's as immense as an ocean, I don't think anyone knows what lies beyond."

"And to the south?" enquired the teacher.

"Desert as far as the eye can see," Robin hesitated again. "Nobody knows what's beyond that either. To the west is the Vast Ocean. It's said to be guarded by sea monsters."

This last statement was met with silence. Each student had formed a mental picture of the world Robin had just been describing, and found that The Lost Isle, despite its mysterious heaths and thick forests, its sorcerers and Korrigans, sounded rather tame in comparison.

"Does anybody want to ask Robin a question?" asked the teacher.

Just then, the bell announcing the end of the school day rang. The teacher dampened the class's excitement by announcing:

"You may not leave until you have copied the sketch of The Uncertain World into your exercise books. There will be a test on it tomorrow!"

There were howls of protest, but they all sat down and hurriedly drew the map.

"Obviously, you are excused from this exercise," he added, turning to Robin. "Thank you for this rather special geography lesson. You may go."

Robin didn't wait to be told twice. He politely took his leave of the teacher and left the room.

He hurried across the playground. The tall beech trees were beginning to take on subtle hues of russet and gold, but he barely glanced at them. He was just about to exit through the gate when he heard a commotion behind him. He turned around and saw Agatha Balangru and Thomas Kandarisar, formerly the two school bullies, laughing and joking loudly, and heading in his direction.

"Robin! There you are!" exclaimed Thomas, a strong, stocky boy with a mop of red hair.

"We've been trying to catch up with you all day," explained Agatha. "I'm having a party at my place this afternoon — it'd be great if you could come!"

Robin gazed at the tall, rather skinny girl who was smiling at him with her disproportionately large mouth. To think that before he'd rescued her from the clutches of Commander Thunku in The Uncertain World, she'd been his archenemy and worst nightmare! And now, Agatha Balangru was falling over herself to be nice to him.

Robin felt his heart beat a little faster.

He looked at her properly for the first time, and noticed that her face was almost pleasant when she wasn't smirking cruelly. It had an easy confidence that made her attractive in her own way.

But Amber's disapproving face popped into Robin's mind and he felt guilty for thinking such things. His feisty friend was less than fond of Agatha.

As for Thomas, the ex-thug he'd saved from a Gommon's knife on a beach of The Lost Isle, he was still Agatha's sidekick. But, since that day, he always gazed at Robin with rapt admiration.

"I'm sorry, Agatha," replied Robin with a sincere sigh. "I'd have loved to, but I have to meet Master Quadehar. He's waiting for me on the heath."

And it was true that the lessons with Quadehar, the Master Sorcerer, had become even more intensive since the start of the new school year, now even taking up his free afternoons.

"No problem," said Agatha, looking disappointed. "Next time, hopefully."

"Yes . . . Have fun!"

Robin waved good-bye with an apologetic smile, then raced off. He was late.

And Master Quadehar didn't like to be kept waiting.

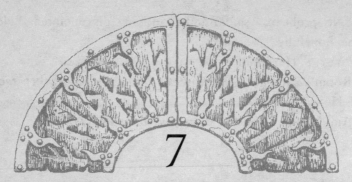

7

A WALK ON THE HEATH

"Another five minutes and I was going to come looking for you!" exclaimed Quadehar the Sorcerer.

Out of breath, Robin had just appeared at the foot of the dolmen, the standing stone, on the slopes of the hills overlooking Dashtikazar where he met his master to work on his art.

"Were you afraid that an Ork might try and kidnap me again?" asked Robin, who was having difficulty catching his breath.

"I'm more afraid that you'll allow yourself to be distracted and forget your lesson!"

Quadehar jumped nimbly down from the huge granite slab where he'd been sitting and waiting for Robin.

He was built like an athlete, with a square face and short hair. His eyes were steel blue and he had a warm voice. The kindly smile that hovered on his lips softened his stern expression. It was difficult to say how old he was — he could be around thirty-five or forty. The dark cloak and canvas bag he always carried indicated that he belonged to the world of magic. Master

Quadehar was the most prominent sorcerer in the Guild and the sworn enemy of The Shadow.

"What are we going to do today, Master?" asked Robin.

"We're going for a walk on the heath. It's a lovely day, so we may as well get some exercise! Naturally, we'll make the most of the opportunity to do a little studying, too."

Robin was pleased with this plan. These walks with his master were often a chance to discuss subjects that were outside the strict framework of his apprenticeship. They set off amid the heather and the gorse. After a while, Quadehar started questioning his apprentice.

"Robin, do you feel that you have fully mastered the twenty-four Graphems?"

"Yes, Master. I simply need to close my eyes and they're there, all glowing."

"Do you make the effort to maintain contact with them every day?"

"Yes, Master. I call them up in my mind by name and they hum and vibrate."

"Do you know how to use the Graphems?"

"I know how to project them, by shouting or whispering their names. I know how to reinforce them, by adopting the Stadha. I know how to combine them and weave them together to compose Galdrs and incantations."

"What is a Galdr?"

"It's a spell using the Graphems like words in a sentence."

"What is a Graphem, Robin?"

"It's a letter of a magic alphabet, written in the stars, which enables you to enter the Wyrd."

"And what is the Wyrd?"

"It's like a giant spider's web whose threads are attached to everything that exists. By opening the Wyrd, the Graphems make it possible to influence all these things."

"What are the sorcerer's two most powerful weapons in the Wyrd?"

"Prudence and humility."

"Now, which is the Graphem of travel?"

"Raidhu, the chariot of Nerthus, the fifth Graphem."

"Are there good and bad Graphems?"

"No. There are only good and bad sorcerers. The Graphems are neutral energies whose effect depends solely on the user. As I know only too well, Master!"

Quadehar smiled, then nodded.

"You have an answer for everything, my boy. It's a vital quality . . . for someone who wants to become a tradesman or a teacher! But for someone who aims to become a sorcerer, it takes a bit more . . ."

The words were barely out of his mouth when he suddenly cried out "Ingwaz!" — then stepped back and instantly adopted the Stadha of Ingwaz and cast the power of the Graphem over the apprentice. Robin reacted promptly. He had seen his Master take up the position of the "freezing" symbol and had anticipated it by adopting the Naudhiz posture, which neutralized magic attacks. He just had the time to call the protective Graphem to his aid. There was a flash of golden light. Quadehar's attack had failed.

"I'm impressed," admitted the sorcerer. "I can see that you're not just talk!"

"*From word to word, the word will guide me. From act to act, the act will guide me*, Master!" Robin grinned cheekily.

It was one of the sayings the sorcerers had laboriously copied from the *Book of the Stars*, a very long time ago.

"Well, well, so you're interested in words of wisdom now?"

The sorcerer, who had resumed a normal posture, was standing a few paces from his pupil. Suddenly, he threw out his hand and made a gesture in Robin's direction.

This time, the apprentice wasn't fast enough and, with a cry of surprise, he found himself glued to the spot.

"How did you do that, Master? You didn't adopt a Stadha, and I didn't hear you call Ingwaz!"

"Oh yes I did, Robin," explained Quadehar, releasing his pupil from the spell he'd cast on him. "But you weren't aware of it. There's a silent way to reinforce or use the Graphems!"

Robin sat down on the ground and took out from his bag the fat black leather-bound notebook in which he wrote down anything that he felt was important.

"Earlier on," continued Quadehar, "you told me that you knew how to use the Graphems, by shouting or whispering them, by adopting Stadha, and by combining them in spells and incantations. Now I'm going to teach you to use them in a different manner, less forceful perhaps, but faster and much more discreet."

"I'm all ears, Master!" Robin encouraged him. He loved these moments when his master stopped trying to drum into him the boring names of plants or complicated wind patterns, and taught him the techniques of real magic instead.

Quadehar drew the shapes of each of the twenty-four Graphems in the air. His movements were swift and animated. At the same time, he explained to his rapt pupil what he was doing. "These are Mudra, movements of the hand in the air that reproduce the shapes of the Graphems. . . . Like the Stadha, the Mudra enable you to call on their powers in silence, or to reinforce them. In the last case, you just need to murmur the name of the Graphem as you draw its shape."

"And what are the advantages and disadvantages of the Mudra, compared with the Stadha?" asked Robin, frowning.

"I told you, the Stadha reinforce the power of the magic. But they're slower and less discreet than the Mudra. Both Stadha and Mudra also help strengthen your Galdrs. For example, the Desert Galdr, which requires a huge amount of energy, couldn't work with Mudra."

"I get it now, Master. If I'm in a hurry, or if I don't want anyone to see me, I use the Mudra. If I need real force, I use the Stadha!"

"You've grasped the basics," acknowledged Quadehar. "The rest will come with practice. Have you sufficiently mastered the Stadha?"

"Yes, Master, I think so."

"Perfect. Now let's deal with the Mudra. Give me your hands . . ."

The sorcerer spent the rest of the afternoon, sitting on the heath, teaching his pupil the magic gestures. When he was certain that Robin had learned them all, he stood up.

"Right. Let's continue our walk, my boy. We've still got some time left, and besides, there's something I need to talk to you about."

≈ ✳ ≈ ✳ ≈

At first, the sorcerer walked along in silence. Beside him, Robin waited patiently for him to speak. It wasn't long before he began.

"Soon, Robin, you will have acquired all the basic elements to begin studying sorcery in more depth."

"When, Master?" asked Robin excitedly.

"I told you — soon," replied Quadehar, who suddenly seemed distracted by something else.

His master's reply disappointed him, but Robin held his tongue and didn't press the matter. They walked on in silence again along the path that crossed Korrigans heath. Then Quadehar went on wearily:

"I know I'm pushing you, Robin. I tell you secrets and teach you practices that an apprentice doesn't usually learn for two or three years, but in my opinion, I judge it's possible, and above all, necessary . . ."

"What do you mean, Master?" asked Robin, intrigued. Quadehar had rarely confided in him like this.

"You are an intelligent boy, Robin. You have a powerful gift for magic, and you know it. Didn't you knock a Gommon senseless and paralyse an Ork? Didn't you open The Door of The Uncertain World and destroy Commander Thunku's palace when you'd been an apprentice for only three months?"

"Yes, but . . . ?"

"Do you remember the difficulties you had with the Graphems in The Uncertain World, because you hadn't modified them according to the stars in that world?"

"Of course I remember, Master. Instead of helping me

concentrate, Isaz froze two thieves! And Thursaz, who was supposed to protect me against Thunku's guards, caused an earthquake."

"That's the whole problem, Robin," sighed Master Quadehar. "You have a tremendous Ond — inner force — but you're not yet able to control it. In teaching you magic, I have awakened this force, but to prevent it from causing further disasters, you'll have to learn to control it."

"And I'm going to have to work very hard, aren't I, Master?"

Robin said this with such a serious expression that the sorcerer couldn't help smiling.

"Yes, my boy. I know it's not easy for you, that you'd rather spend the time enjoying yourself with your friends. But you and I have a responsibility toward the magic powers. And we are bound by a pledge made under oath: I to teach you magic, and you to learn it."

Robin visualized himself as if it were yesterday, shaking the sorcerer's hand, mingling the symbols of patience and obedience drawn on their palms with yew charcoal. He had never questioned that commitment. In becoming an apprentice, he had at last found his place. To his friends and schoolmates and to all those strangers who recognized him, he was Robin the apprentice sorcerer who had rescued Thomas from the clutches of a Gommon and Agatha from the dreaded Uncertain World. He realized he had new responsibilities, and his first obligation was to pursue his apprenticeship diligently. He knew this, and accepted it. So he was surprised that his master was evoking their oath now.

"I know all that, Master. Why do you mention it?"

"An expedition involving the Guild's best sorcerers," explained

Quadehar after a brief pause, "will be setting off for The Uncertain World to storm The Shadow's lair . . ."

"You told me that too, Master," replied Robin surprised. "But what you haven't told me," he went on hopefully, "is where The Shadow hides himself in The Uncertain World."

"That's irrelevant, at least as far as you're concerned," replied Quadehar with an evasive wave of his hand. "On the other hand, what I didn't tell you, Robin, is that during the attack you'll be sent to the Monastery of Gifdu for your safety. No, don't protest, it's useless! I understand that you have unpleasant memories of that place, but our Chief Sorcerer, Charfalaq, has decided it's best. Besides, the Provost and even your mother agree that it is a reasonable precaution. Who knows how The Shadow will react to our attack?"

Robin opened his mouth to argue, but Quadehar's authoritative tone dissuaded him. How awful! He would soon be shut up in Gifdu, which he'd had to escape from last time to meet up with his friends. He knew he'd probably have to go back there one day, but he hadn't expected it to be so soon, or in these circumstances. He mentally cursed Charfalaq, that sly old dodderer who made his flesh creep, and was now forcing him to return to the monastery.

He calculated the number of days left before the Samain holidays. Whew, there was plenty of time. He would be back in Dashtikazar to spend the holidays with Romaric, Godfrey, Amber, and Coral. And if he wasn't, he'd just have to run away again!

The thought of seeing Gerald, the laid-back computer wizard, and Qadwan, the elderly gymnasium master, cheered him up a little. Robin turned to Quadehar, "When do I leave?"

"We'll set out this evening, after you've packed your bag and said good-bye to your mother, and I've been to your uncle's to borrow a horse."

"That soon?" exclaimed Robin. "But why? What's going on?"

"After consulting the stars, Charfalaq has decided to move up the attack on The Shadow. It was planned for next month, but now it will take place within the next few days."

8

BERTRAM

Robin was less than overjoyed to find himself and his master once more sharing a little guest room on one of the upper floors of the monastery. It was like the one they'd had before, on his previous stay at Gifdu — simple and clean, with two beds, a table, two chairs, and an adjoining bathroom. The difference was that this room was not on the third floor of the south wing with a view over the gorge. After his daring escape with a rope the previous summer, they'd been careful to give him a room that didn't open onto the outside wall.

The window of this second-floor room overlooked the cloistered inner courtyard facing the massive main entrance where the sorcerers liked to stroll and chat.

As before, Robin soon felt lonely. His master was very much in demand and was always rushing off to meetings. Thirty of the Guild's most powerful sorcerers had been chosen to carry out an attack on The Shadow, and Quadehar had been appointed leader. And so the Monastery of Gifdu, the Guild's headquarters, was a hive of activity. Robin had noticed it immediately; preoccupied sorcerers thronged the corridors, and Gerald, the computer wizard who he'd gotten along with so well before, merely gave him a cursory wave by way of a greeting. Even Qadwan, the elderly sorcerer in charge of the gym, had no time for Robin. The only person who seemed to appreciate his dropping in was Eugene, the sorcerer responsible for the monastery's mailroom, which was submerged by avalanches of mail during this busy period.

To fend off boredom and the disappointment of being excluded from the preparations for the expedition, Robin devoted an hour or two to sorting through the letters and packages before heading off to the libraries again. He made his way down corridors that only the Talking Stones — carved stones that literally gave directions — made it possible to tell apart. The monastery was vast, both above and below ground, and its corridors were a real labyrinth. Apprentices on their first visit were always getting lost, until they discovered how to use the Talking Stones.

≋ ✳ ≋ ✳ ≋

This particular morning, Robin lingered in the library of The Uncertain World. He had spent a lot of time there last summer planning his getaway; not a single book on the metal shelves of the smallest room had escaped his inquisitive eyes.

Now, in the vast paneled room of the history library, he read a chapter on the history of Gifdu and discovered that the monastery had been built five hundred years before Dashtikazar, the thousand-year-old capital of The Lost Isle.

Then he wandered into the natural history library, which was filled with stuffed animals. He settled down and watched a documentary on seagulls. On leaving the room, he bumped into a sorcerer in a great hurry, nearly knocking him over.

"Whoops! Sorry!"

"Don't worry, but next time look where you're going!"

Robin was intrigued by the young man who was adjusting his shirt collar. His sorcerer's cloak was immaculate and looked brand-new. Of average height, he was solidly built and looked about sixteen. He wore his longish hair brushed back and, unusually for The Lost Isle, he had a goatee and a thin moustache. There was a mocking glint in his dark eyes and an ironic smile hovered on his lips. Robin looked him up and down.

"Are you new? I haven't met you before?" Robin asked, staring openly at him.

There was a hint of sarcasm in the young sorcerer's voice as he replied: "I've never seen you before either. Mind you, that's hardly surprising given your size."

"Oh, I wouldn't trust appearances," retorted Robin, undaunted by the young man's superior air. "Look at Charfalaq, our Chief Sorcerer — he looks like a doddery old thing, but he's a truly powerful sorcerer!"

The young sorcerer was speechless for a moment and then he burst out laughing. He gave Robin a friendly clap on the back. "A kid with a real sense of humor. Charfalaq is a doddery old thing indeed. . . . You wouldn't be the famous Robin by any chance, would you?"

"I hope you don't believe everything you've heard. . . ."

"Until now, yes. But people say you're as big as a bear and your eyes flash lightning. . . . I'll be more critical from now on!"

"Don't be so quick to judge," Robin retorted. "As big as a bear maybe not, but as for the flashes . . ."

"Oh, I'd better watch out, then, but I don't *think* you scare me. I'm Bertram, by the way." He smiled, proffering his hand which Robin shook firmly.

"Delighted to meet you, if I may say so," replied Robin, imitating Gerald, who had greeted him with those words on his first visit to the monastery.

"You can cut that out, too! For your information, Gerald is . . . or rather was, my master sorcerer for five years!"

"For five years? I thought it only took three years to become a fully qualified sorcerer."

"Hey! Show some respect," said Bertram. "Gerald is a harsh master, much tougher than all the others and he's seen fit to train me for five years. Not like Quadehar, for example, who's a real softy and will let you off with three. . . ."

"I don't believe a word of it," declared Robin with an earnestness that disconcerted the newly ordained sorcerer momentarily. "Tell me the truth."

"The truth, you presumptuous little apprentice, is that I have everything it takes to be a very great sorcerer, and that's a fact. Only Gerald deemed me to be . . . how shall I put it . . . a little too wild. A crazy young pup! That's what he used to say during my apprenticeship."

"And what made him change his mind?"

"The fear that I might turn around and bite him!"

"Oh, come on, let's have the real reason," said Robin, looking him straight in the eye. "I don't buy that."

Bertram stared at the boy standing before him and, for a fleeting second, he had the feeling that he was the apprentice and Robin the sorcerer. He shook his shoulders to rid himself of that unpleasant feeling.

"And why should I have to explain myself to a kid?"

"I don't know," said Robin, knitting his brow. "Perhaps because I am the only person apart from Gerald who can see your talent underneath all that unpleasantness."

"Well, I'm bowled over!" exclaimed Bertram. "Precocious little brat!"

It was a long time since anyone had got the better of Bertram like that. And the worst part was, that he simply couldn't bring himself to be angry. . . .

"OK," agreed Bertram. "All right! Fair's fair. If we're going to exchange secrets, let's make a friendship pact. Give me your hand . . ."

Robin held out his hand without hesitation. Bertram took a stick of yew charcoal out of his bag and drew the symbol of friendship on Robin's palm. He did likewise on his own. Then they shook hands vigorously, smudging the charcoal on their hands.

"So come on, now we're officially friends," Robin said. "Why did Gerald change his mind and let you take the sorcerer's oath?"

"Because I promised to be good," replied Bertram with a wink.

Robin had the feeling he'd been fooled, but before he could reply they were interrupted by Eugene, who couldn't cope with the staggering mail delivery that had arrived and needed his help.

Robin left Bertram, arranging to meet him in the refectory for dinner, determined to get more out of the infuriating sorcerer. Following Eugene to the pigeon house that was the monastery's mailroom, he realized that his stay at Gifdu promised to be less boring than he'd expected now that he'd met Bertram.

9

MONKEY BUSINESS

At meal times, the monastery guests who had not opted to dine quietly in their rooms sat in groups around the wooden tables in the refectory. Sorcerers and apprentices went up and helped themselves as often as they pleased from the counter where the chef arranged an array of dishes.

Bertram and Robin were sitting at the same table, with a sorcerer from the other end of The Lost Isle. He had come to show Gifdu to his apprentice, who sat staring at everything round-eyed.

After wolfing down a whole serving of chicken and peas, Bertram leaned over toward Robin:

"Watch this!"

He formed a discreet Mudra and invoked Laukaz, the hook-shaped Graphem used in all growth processes, and directed it toward the chair of the Bursar of Gifdu, a tall, bearded man with a stern expression. Immediately, the seat rose one foot higher, raising the sorcerer above the table.

"Who did that? Who did that?" roared the Bursar while his neighbors helped him down, trying to stifle their laughter.

Bertram bowed his head, trying to conceal a wicked grin. Opposite him, the sorcerer from the provinces and his apprentice had eyes only for the furious man with the beard.

It's unbelievable, Robin thought, taken aback. *He's about as mature as a first-year apprentice! How on earth could Gerald have allowed him to become a sorcerer?*

"It's to get my own back for all the humiliations that old devil has inflicted on me," explained Bertram in a whisper to Robin. "Come on, let's not hang around here any longer."

Robin hesitated for a moment, but on seeing the way the Bursar was glaring at him, he hurried out of the room on the heels of his new friend. He'd been on the Bursar's bad side since the incident of the fake Talking Stone he'd made out of papier-mâché, which had directed a group of apprentices to the laundry room in the basement.

"I thought you weren't allowed to use magic against other sorcerers," Robin said in amazement, as soon as they were out of earshot.

"It's no fun sticking to the rules," grumbled Bertram, smoothing his hair back. "Anyway, if what they say about you is true, you're hardly in a position to lecture me!"

Robin thought for a moment before replying. He himself was only an apprentice, whereas Bertram was, officially at least, a full-fledged sorcerer. OK, so a young sorcerer in training, but he was still a sorcerer. He kept his thoughts to himself and went along with Bertram's argument.

"Perhaps you're right. But all the same, that poor Bursar . . ."

"It won't kill him! Besides, he's made me uncomfortable plenty of times so it serves him right. That's enough of that. Follow me, I'm going to show you something absolutely amazing!"

"Really? What?"

"Wait and see."

They walked along the corridors side by side, Bertram swaggering along and Robin, as usual, lost in thought. There was something else about Bertram that fascinated Robin. It was his accent, which wasn't like any of the accents of The Lost Isle. The apprentice decided to ask him about it outright.

"Hey, Bertram, which part of The Lost Isle are you from?"

Bertram hesitated for a fraction of a second, then replied, "From some godforsaken dump, probably just like you. There's nothing but godforsaken dumps on The Lost Isle. Apparently, they're called villages. . . ."

"You're avoiding the question. I already told you, I won't let you get away with being evasive."

"I come from the tiny village of Jaggar, in the Golden Mountains. Satisfied?"

Bertram was walking faster, and seemed annoyed. Robin bit his tongue. The little village of Jaggar had been decimated by The Shadow's troops a few years back, shortly before the Knights of the Wind had driven the Orks and their master back to the darkness of The Uncertain World. Bertram probably had relatives and friends among the heaps of dead left in their wake.

Great, Robin, he scolded himself. *You had to put your foot in your mouth!*

He caught up with the young sorcerer.

"Er . . . I'm sorry, Bertram. I apologize. I shouldn't have . . ."

"Forget it. There's nothing you can do about it. Me, neither."

Bertram was soon back to his arrogant self, his exasperating expression firmly in place again. Robin was just glad to see him back to normal. Suddenly, Bertram motioned for him to be quiet. They tiptoed in silence up to a half-open door that led into a vast hall.

Inside, Quadehar and the sorcerers chosen to carry out the attack on The Shadow were tirelessly practicing postures and movements.

"What are they doing?" asked Robin, who was fascinated by what he was witnessing.

"They're training to master the Graphems of The Uncertain World. Remember, our Graphems don't work in the same way there. . . ."

"Yes, I know," Robin broke in. "When I tried to project Thursaz, I unleashed an earthquake!"

Bertram gazed at the apprentice with new admiration.

"Gerald told me that you had the most powerful Ond he'd ever seen."

"That's what Master Quadehar said, too," added Robin modestly. "You know, it's nothing to do with me! Apparently, I was just born like that."

"Wow, what luck! If I only had half your magic gift, with my talents I'd be the most powerful sorcerer in the Guild!"

Robin was staggered by his friend's conceit. *What a bighead*, he thought. Although he found Bertram's boldness funny, his overconfidence was breathtaking!

"Pride goes before a fall," Robin replied.

"It's not pride, it's the truth!" protested Bertram. "You'll see, I'm a pretty great sorcerer, believe me!"

"Making the legs of a chair in a refectory grow is no big deal," objected Robin. "Listen, Bertram. I want to be your friend, but on the condition that you stop bragging. Take my word, it's very dangerous to forget that *prudence* . . ."

". . . *and humility are the sorcerer's motto*! Back off, will you? You sound like my master!"

"Well, you might have heard his words, but you weren't listening properly," retorted Robin. "If you'd been through what I've been through, you'd agree with me. You don't mess around with the Wyrd!"

This time, Bertram was speechless. He stared at Robin who stood confronting him, trembling with emotion, with his fists clenched by his sides, and he suddenly felt small in front of the apprentice. This boy had obviously experienced some terrible things! Things that had perhaps forced him to grow up too quickly. . . .

"OK," admitted the young sorcerer. "You're right. Some things are sacred."

A smile lit up Robin's face.

"That's not exactly what I meant," he said, winking at Bertram. "You can make fun of most things, but there are certain things that *are* off limits."

Just then, Quadehar, noticing their presence, put an end to their philosophical discussion by sending them to their rooms. They knew from the tone of his voice that there was no point in arguing. The apprentice and the junior sorcerer crept off without a word.

10

A Stolen Lesson

Robin couldn't get to sleep. He thrashed around in his bed, trying in vain to find a position that would allow him to drop off. He glanced over to his master's bed. Quadehar still wasn't back. He was probably working late with the sorcerers in the hall.

Why didn't Master Quadehar take advantage of this unique opportunity to keep Robin with him? After all, he was his apprentice. And it was an excellent way to teach him all sorts of things!

Robin tossed this way and that, seeking a cooler spot on his pillow. He felt so frustrated. Of course, Master Quadehar had his reasons. He had even explained them to him: He was afraid of pushing Robin too fast when it came to magic. But it really didn't make sense because he was also concerned that Robin didn't have enough knowledge or experience to control his power! Robin fidgeted for a while longer, then, suddenly, he sat up. His mind was made up: He'd go down to the training hall and take a peek. Just a peek.

≈ ✳ ≈ ✳ ≈

Robin got dressed, grabbed a candle, and left the room without making a sound. He tiptoed down the corridors, keeping close to the wall and pausing at each intersection, his heart pounding. He certainly didn't want to have to explain to the Bursar what he was doing skulking in the corridors at this late hour! He cupped his hand to protect the little flame of the candle, which cast its flickering light onto the ceiling. Luckily, it was late and he didn't bump into anyone.

He soon reached the door of the hall — it stood ajar, sending a thin shaft of light across the floor. Holding his breath, he peeked inside.

The sorcerers were all there, gathered around Quadehar. They looked tired from the day's exercises. They were arguing. One of them, an animated man dressed in a voluminous dark cloak, turned to Quadehar. "What happens, Quadehar, if I'm attacked by The Shadow himself or by one of his henchmen?"

"You start praying!" burst out another sorcerer.

There was general laughter. They clearly needed to unwind.

"Go on, Ulriq," Quadehar encouraged him.

"I was wondering," continued the sorcerer, "if it would be better, in The Uncertain World, to use the Armor of Elhaz or the Helmet of Terror for protection against a physical attack or against magic?"

Robin pricked up his ears. Elhaz? That was the fifteenth Graphem in the alphabet. It thawed difficult situations and opened locks. He had never been aware that it could be used to protect against magic.

"That's a very good question," replied Quadehar. "As you know," he went on addressing the company, "Elhaz offers protection against magic when it is used as a Galdr or a Lokk. In the event of a physical or magic attack, using the Armor of Elhaz as a shield is the best protection you can have. Even in The Uncertain World."

Quadehar repositioned himself so that all the sorcerers could see him.

A Lokk? What's a Lokk? Robin silently wondered. *I'll have to ask Bertram.*

"The Armor of Elhaz," continued Quadehar, matching his words with actions, "is created by joining Elhaz to itself six times in a Galdr. This applies both here and in The Uncertain World — but bear in mind that the Graphems there take on different shapes. You visualize Elhaz, then you draw it six times in the air or on the ground. The incantation remains unchanged: *By the power of Erda and Kari, Rind, Hir, and Loge, Elhaz in front, Elhaz behind, Elhaz to the left, Elhaz to the right, Elhaz above and Elhaz below, Elhaz protect me! ALU!*"

Quadehar, who had drawn the symbols in the dust and uttered the magic words, was immediately protected by a force field that seemed to form an invisible wall on which some of the sorcerers rapped with their knuckles. Robin was bewildered.

"We all know about the Armor of Elhaz," said one sorcerer. "But will it be any use where we're going?"

"Yes," replied Quadehar, rubbing out the Graphems drawn on the floor and removing the protective barrier. "As long as you draw the Uncertain Elhaz correctly, which is not so easy. And that's why I advise you not to seek the protection of Elhaz by donning the Helmet of Terror until you have completely mastered the Uncertain Graphems!"

"But the Helmet is much more powerful than the Armor," retorted a strapping fellow whose sorcerer's cloak was too short for him.

"That's true," admitted Quadehar. "But it is also more complex to execute. Let me explain: The Helmet of Terror is obtained by mixing Elhaz eight times with itself in a Lokk; to do that, either in the air above your head or on the ground, you draw eight blurred Elhaz to form an eight-point star, each point ending in a trident. This forms a new Graphem, Egishjamur, which is more solid, because it is unique and more concentrated than the six Elhaz combined in the Armor Galdr. . . . But if just one of the eight Elhaz isn't drawn properly, that's enough to invalidate the Lokk. Whereas if one of the six Elhaz for the Armor is badly drawn, the Galdr will still function, although it may be a bit weak."

Quadehar gave a demonstration, using Mudra to trace the shapes of a perfect Helmet of Terror and a second shaky one, then a perfect Armor and another wobbly one. Thus the sorcerers were able to see for themselves that he knew what he was talking about. Concealed behind the doorpost, Robin didn't miss a word of this riveting lesson.

"So, Quadehar," concluded the sorcerer Ulriq, "you advise us to use the Galdr rather than the Lokk in The Uncertain World?"

"If you're asking the question, it's because you don't have sufficient experience, so my advice is, keep it simple! And the Galdr is always simpler than the Lokk. Now, my friends, it's late, and my only remaining advice is: Go to bed. We have a tough day ahead of us tomorrow!"

They all laughed and nodded. Then they headed for the door in small clusters, discussing Quadehar's lesson. He was the only one who had already been to the terrible World which they were preparing to invade.

The minute he heard Master Quadehar dismiss the sorcerers, Robin scampered back to his room. He hadn't grasped everything he'd overheard during his stolen lesson, but he had understood enough to open up new prospects for his magic! By extracting the missing information from various sources, he would soon move on to a new level in his initiation, with or without the help of his master.

Quadehar entered the room noiselessly and went to bed, taking care not to rouse his pupil, unaware that he was wide awake. Robin, meanwhile, was carefully stowing away in his memory everything he had seen and heard that night, and it was ages before he finally fell asleep.

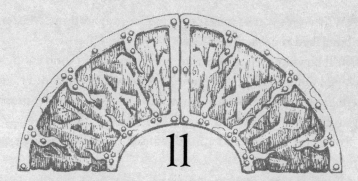

11
BEFORE SETTING OFF

The next day, Robin was wandering around the monastery in search of Bertram when Qadwan came running up to him, slightly out of breath.

"I've been looking for you for the last hour," grumbled the old man.

"What's wrong?" asked Robin.

"It's Quadehar; he's waiting for you in your room. His departure is now set for tomorrow, and he wants to see you before he leaves."

Robin thanked the sorcerer and raced up the stairs.

≋ ✳ ≋ ✳ ≋

"You wanted to see me, Master?" asked Robin, entering the room where Quadehar sat waiting for him on one of the twin beds.

"Yes, Robin. I've managed to take some time off from our preparations for the attack. We can make the most of it to do some work."

"Why won't you let me take part in the preparations, Master?" Robin asked reproachfully.

"It'll be your turn to confront the enemy again soon enough," snapped Quadehar. "Enjoy your freedom while you can! Besides, there are several types of preparations. You can start by preparing to become a sorcerer!"

Robin bit his lip and forced himself to look obedient and attentive.

"What are we going to do today?"

"We're going to practice fixing the Graphems."

From his bag, the sorcerer took out a strange short dagger with a sharp blade. He held it out to Robin who grabbed it eagerly.

"This is a Ristir, an engraving dagger. It is used for fixing the Graphems. Of course, you can use it for stabbing an attacker in the neck if you haven't got the time or the opportunity to invoke the Graphems! But that's something different. . . ."

"What a beautiful object, Master!" exclaimed Robin, gazing raptly at the dagger.

"Yes, but above all it's very useful! Whether you shout, whisper, or draw them in the air, eventually the Graphems will disappear. They are mainly effective as soon as they are released. If you want them to last longer, you have to fix them by etching them . . . that's why they are carved on the door of the monastery and on The Doors to the Two Worlds! Now, take this Ristir and etch Graphems one, two, three, five, eight, ten, eleven, thirteen, fourteen, fifteen, twenty-two, and twenty-three on the floor."

Robin grasped the engraving dagger and carefully drew on the floor the Graphems his master had chosen from the alphabet of the stars.

"Fehu, Great Wealth, Uruz the Russet Cow; Thursaz the Antelope and the Thorn; Raidhu the Chariot of Nerthus; Wunjo the Standard and the Way; Naudhiz the Spark and the Hand; Isaz the Brilliant and Ice; Eiwaz the Ancient Tree and the Double Branch; Perthro the Dice Cup; Elhaz the Ancestor and the Swan; Ingwaz the Wealthy and the Nail; Dagaz, Daylight . . ." murmured Robin as he drew the shapes of the Graphems in the dust.

"Good," said Quadehar, after watching Robin's precise, confident movements. "A Galdr can be fixed in the same way. Now listen carefully: Each Graphem, as you know, has one or more powers. When you call it up, either orally or by drawing it in the air or on the ground, these powers have a simple, direct effect. The Galdr combines the Graphems in order to obtain a more complex result. So, to use The Doors to the other worlds, the Travel Graphem alone isn't sufficient. Nor is the Graphem of Communication between the worlds, or the Graphem of Cohesion. If you throw the separate ideas: *I have a vehicle and I want to set off on a journey*, *I want to communicate between the worlds*, and *We'll stay together*, one by one against The Door, you certainly won't end up in The Uncertain World! On the other hand, if you weave all these words together to make up a coherent sentence, along the lines of: *I have a vehicle and I want to set off on a journey with my friends, and so I need to establish communication* — now, that way you'll arrive in The Uncertain World with your friends. It's just like putting the *words* together in the correct way. So in our magic sentence everything will work together, too — as long as you don't forget one of the three Graphems in your Galdr!"

Robin flushed crimson. His master was alluding to the mistake he'd made last summer, when he'd opened The Door to The Uncertain World . . . Robin felt ashamed, even though Quadehar wasn't really making fun of him. He was simply reminding him that you had to be vigilant in handling the Graphems.

Soon, the sorcerer rose to leave, visibly satisfied that his pupil had learned the lesson so quickly. But Robin grabbed his sleeve.

"Master, please . . ."

"What is it, Robin?"

"I heard somebody talking about Lokks. What are they?"

"Who told you about them?"

Robin hesitated for a moment, then he replied, "Bertram, Master."

Quadehar shook his head disapprovingly.

"I was planning to teach you that aspect of the magic of the stars later," he said, "but since you're curious, I'll answer your question, without going into too much detail. It's a bit complicated, and anyway, you don't need it for the moment."

The sorcerer sat down again.

"Listen, Robin, in addition to the Galdr, there's another way of combining the Graphems, and that is the Lokk. The Galdr weaves together and links the Graphems, makes a sentence out of the words, whereas the Lokk blends and mixes the Graphems and creates a new word. The Galdr combines powers by adding them together, while the Lokk mixes these powers to obtain a new power. . . . That probably sounds a bit confusing, doesn't it?"

"Yes, Master," admitted Robin.

"So, imagine that the Graphems are little stones, and that your magic aim is to break a glass wall that's imprisoning you. Using a single Graphem would be like throwing one little stone at the wall. If the glass is very thin, in other words, if your objective is very simple, it might be sufficient to break it. Are you with me?"

"Yes, Master."

"But if the wall is thicker, the little stone won't be enough. So you'll have to make a Galdr, in other words, throw a handful of stones at the glass wall. That might do the job. But if it's really thick, the little stones will bounce off. Am I making myself clear?"

"Clear as glass, Master!"

"Hmm . . . little monkey! So how are you going to break the glass? By creating a Lokk, and taking several little stones and turning them into a big rock! Like little balls of modeling clay that you stick together to make one big ball! Because if you throw a big stone at the glass wall, instead of one or several little stones, there's a good chance that you'll smash it . . . and be able to escape! That's the principle of the Lokk, compared to the Graphem used on its own, and compared to the Galdr! Do you understand?"

"I understand," replied Robin.

He was delighted. He had obtained the answer to his questions without arousing his master's suspicions. Now, he held several keys: All he had to do was set to work.

"You can't imagine the possibilities that will open up for you when I've finished teaching you," Quadehar went on. "With the twenty-four Graphems of the star alphabet, and the basic spells that you'll have learned, you will be free to make up your own magic! To mix or combine, call, draw in the air, or etch the keys to the Wyrd, as you please and according to your need! Of course, you'll always bear in mind that . . . what, Robin?"

"That *prudence and humility govern the sorcerer's actions.*"

"Absolutely! And never forget the warnings of the apprentice's Poem of Wisdom: *Know how . . .*"

"*. . . to write and to interpret,*
Feel the colors and the shapes
When to cast and when to cast off,
Then know your Graphem's measured fate.
Sometimes it's better not to ask the question
When the answer's in the Stars
Feel the strength as it grows within you
And find your gift will reap its own reward."

"Well done, Robin. Now, off with you. I've got to go and join the other sorcerers."

Robin didn't hang around. It was nearly dinnertime! He reached the door, then paused and turned to Quadehar, who had risen to his feet.

"Master?"

"Yes, Robin."

"Take good care of yourself tomorrow."

"I promise you I will, my boy."

Robin felt his eyes go misty. Then he chided himself: What on earth must his master think? He waved at Quadehar and hurried off to meet Bertram in the refectory.

12

REVELATION

The next day, at dawn, the thirty representatives of the Guild handpicked to invade The Uncertain World assembled in the gym. Of course, Robin and Bertram were there, together with everyone else who was staying at Gifdu. Who would want to miss such an occasion? The sorcerers taking part in the expedition, equipped with their bags full of instruments and books, looked magnificent in their dark cloaks. There was no doubt that The Shadow was a formidable enemy, and they had to be fully prepared as nothing could be left to chance.

"I don't think I've ever seen anything like this!" Bertram whispered to Robin. "All the greatest sorcerers gathered together!"

"Really?" Robin said sarcastically. "But I don't see you among them!"

"Very funny!"

A commotion at the door made them turn around: The Chief Sorcerer, Charfalaq, supreme head of the Guild, was also coming to see the expedition off. The elderly man, almost blind and bent double, with his face concealed beneath the hood of his cloak, shuffled slowly toward Quadehar with the help of a stick. Even though this man was the Chief Sorcerer, to whom all owed courtesy and respect, Robin disliked him intensely. Perhaps it was because last summer the old sorcerer had wanted to keep him at the monastery against his will. But that incident aside, and without being able to explain why, there was something about the old sorcerer that disquieted him.

Taking Quadehar's hand in his gnarled grip, Charfalaq addressed the men assembled in the gym.

"Sorcerers of the Guild," he began in his rasping voice, "today is a great day. I hope we will at last put an end to the menace of The Shadow who has terrorized our Lost Isle for far too long."

The old man was overcome by a prolonged coughing fit.

"I have appointed Quadehar to command the attack," he went on. "None other is worthy of such an honor."

Applause broke out on all sides. Charfalaq raised his arm, and, by way of a blessing, drew Kenaz, the Graphem of fire, and pushed it toward the group of sorcerers about to leave. Then he withdrew. The sorcerers gathered around and took each other's hands to form a chain. Quadehar, at the head, meticulously imitated by the others, rapidly adopted eight successive postures corresponding to eight Graphems. In unison, they chanted the Galdr corresponding to the sequence. The last word was still echoing when the gym lit up with a blinding flash and the thirty sorcerers disappeared into thin air as if sucked suddenly into the void, right in front of the spectators' astonished eyes.

≈ ✳ ≈ ✳ ≈

Once the expedition had left, everybody went back to their own activities. Charfalaq disappeared, Eugene went back to the monastery's pigeon house, and Qadwan regained possession of his gym. As for Robin, deserted by his master, he chose to stay close to Bertram, who accepted his company, but not without protesting loudly that he wasn't a baby-sitter. He said that if they hadn't sealed their friendship with a pact, he'd happily have told Robin to get lost. But deep down, the young sorcerer was delighted.

"That Desert Galdr was rather surprising," Bertram told Robin, referring to the sorcerers' departure. "It's the first time I've seen it work."

The two boys headed toward the computer room.

"It's so useful!" replied Robin. "With that Galdr, there's no need for a Door anymore! You calculate your journey precisely and move from one World to another, as easily as you'd travel from one end of The Lost Isle to the other!"

"Have you ever seen anyone do that on The Lost Isle?" asked Bertram in surprise, knitting his brow.

"Yes — my master. One day, he came to my rescue by entering a tree and coming out of a rock, more than a mile away."

"In theory," admitted Bertram, "I know how to do it, too, but I've never tried. . . ."

"Quadehar said you need incredibly thorough knowledge of the Wyrd to pull it off. It's not advisable for apprentices or young sorcerers to try it!"

They both laughed. Reaching an intersection, they checked their direction on a Talking Stone.

"All the same," Bertram went on, "I'm a little upset at being left behind, while other sorcerers are risking their lives against Lord Sha!"

Robin thought his heart had stopped.

"What did you say?" he asked Bertram in a quavering voice. "Lord Sha?"

"Yes, really, Lord Sha! Of the Tower of Jaghatel. Didn't you know they say he's The Shadow?"

"The Shadow? What do you mean, The Shadow?" gasped Robin.

"That's the conclusion Charfalaq has come to," explained Bertram, eyeing Robin warily. "From the descriptions given by your friend Godfrey, the banjo player who risked his life escaping from the Tower of Jaghatel, it's thought that the tower is likely The Shadow's stronghold. And as the person who lives there, Lord Sha, is a great friend of Thunku, the man who sent Gommons and Orks to kidnap you, Charfalaq believes that Sha and The Shadow are one and the same person. . . . Why does that upset you?"

Robin didn't feel like answering. He was deeply disturbed by this news. Since Agatha, on returning from The Uncertain World, had told Robin that Lord Sha was looking for a boy of his age who might be his son, he had allowed himself to imagine all sorts of things, even the craziest possibilities, without daring to mention it to his master, and even less to his mother! He often spent whole nights wondering whether they weren't lying to him about his real father. He hadn't reached a satisfactory conclusion. . . . But to discover that his master was going to hunt down this mysterious Lord Sha, who was perhaps The Shadow, but who certainly might know something about where he, Robin, came from, was profoundly distressing.

He sat down on the ground and put his head in his hands, while the astonished Bertram tried to comfort him.

≋ ✳ ≋ ✳ ≋

"I'm here, Master. You wanted to see me?"

"Yes, Lomgo . . . my faithful scribe . . . I have to write two letters . . . two very important letters . . ."

Without showing any visible emotion, the beady-eyed servant watched the blurred form moving about in the recesses of the gray-walled room. Tables were strewn with maps and scribbled sheets of paper; instruments and books were scattered over the floor. Lately, the Master had been prone to frequent fits of excitement that were totally out of character, and even Lomgo, who was considered his confidant, was unaware of the cause. He suspected that his master's elation was in some way linked to the boy he'd been seeking for years, and whom he had found at last. But it was difficult to tell with the Master.

The silhouette enveloped in shadows advanced toward the scribe, who remained impassive in his long, white tunic. The man's bare, shaven head gleamed in the light given off by the torches, their flames flickering as the Master walked past.

"Lomgo . . . you won't be forgotten when my moment of triumph comes. . . . Faithful, yes, faithful scribe . . ."

The powerful, hollow voice that made all the servants quake in their shoes had become honeyed, and Lomgo was flattered. He took a few steps in the direction of a chair closest to the only skylight in the room, where he always sat to take dictation from his master. He opened his writing case with a hand that was missing one finger, and grabbed a quill.

"First of all, we're going to write to Thunku. . . . Then we'll write to our friend . . . our old friend, who feels very much alone in his tower. . . ."

The Master gave a strangled laugh — the first for a very long while. It was enough to send shivers down Lomgo's spine.

13

THE BATTLE OF JAGHATEL

The thirty sorcerers emerged in the ruins of the former city of Jaghatel. Sheltered by the walls of a house that had caved in, they took in their surroundings. Their arrival in The Uncertain World had apparently not been noticed.

There was even a terrifying calm. A deathly silence. The sea birds, usually so noisy, were silent. This atmosphere soon became oppressive. Quadehar lost no time thinking — they must act quickly. He gave a few last-minute orders, and the sorcerers set off for the huge tower that stood dark and menacing on the cliffs, with a sheer drop below into the Vast Ocean.

But, as they drew nearer to their enemy's lair, their apprehension only increased. They couldn't help glancing anxiously about them.

This silence is odd, thought Quadehar. *And it's all too easy. The Shadow's no novice who can be easily caught off guard! What's he waiting for — to counter our attack with an evil spell? I don't like this!*

They reached the foot of the tower, and stood before the only entrance. The door was firmly bolted and protected by a power-ful spell. The silence, broken only by the rhythmic sound of the waves pounding against the rocks below, was still overwhelm-ing. They stepped back to get a better view of the tower.

The sorcerer Ulriq went over to Quadehar. "You're familiar with this World; do you know what this means?"

"I haven't the faintest idea," confessed Quadehar. "But some-thing is indeed amiss."

"Do you think The Shadow heard us coming and has fled?"

"That wouldn't be the worst thing that could happen," Quadehar admitted, scrutinizing the tower.

All down one side of the tower were spiral beams built into the wall like a giant twisty slide.

"That must be how Godfrey escaped," Quadehar softly whis-pered to the sorcerers who had formed a circle around him. "Breaking down the door would take us too long. We'll simply climb up the side and enter the tower from above."

That instant, there was a deafening roar behind them. The sor-cerers swung around in unison and instinctively adopted the Stadha of Naudhiz, the Graphem for resisting attack.

"Remember, friends, we're in The Uncertain World!" yelled Quadehar, watching his colleagues.

To control the magic alphabet in The Uncertain World, there were a number of adjustments to be made; the Graphems had to be modified according to the different forms of the constellations in this other World.

The sorcerers adopted the correct posture, and waited reso-lutely for the attack by what they imagined to be The Shadow.

But the creatures bursting from the ruins and rushing toward them bore no resemblance to a shadow. . . .

"Orks and Hybrids, hundreds of them!" shouted one of the sorcerers. "But where are they coming from?"

"It's a trap!" groaned Quadehar. "They were expecting us!"

And true enough, from the ancient city, a horde of Orks, giant creatures built for killing and maiming, and Hybrids, a cross between Ork and human, were rushing at them bellowing and brandishing axes and clubs.

Quadehar swiftly assessed the situation. They were completely surrounded by the monsters. The sorcerers were herded up against the tower, and then there was nothing between them and the ocean.

"We're surrounded!" shouted Quadehar. "We must face them and fight!"

The sorcerers responded at once. They held back the first wave of attackers by bombarding them with spells. Some invoked Ingwaz to freeze the Orks on the spot, while others called on Thursaz to knock them out. But strangely, even though some of the beasts swayed or looked a little dazed, the Graphems seemed to have little effect on them. The Guild's magic was impotent!

"What can be the reason for this?" wondered Quadehar desperately as, right beside him, a sorcerer was brutally clubbed over the head.

"By the spirits of Gifdu!" raged the Master Sorcerer, neatly leaping out of the way of a charging Ork. Suddenly, his attention was drawn to the medallions that all of the Orks were wearing around their necks. Medallions sporting Commander Thunku's coat of arms, a roaring lion surrounded by flames. The blazon gave off an eerie white glow.

At once, Quadehar understood and turned ashen.

"Watch out!" he yelled to his companions. "The monsters are wearing talismans to protect them from our Graphems!"

Just then, an Ork ran its sword through a sorcerer's stomach and he crumpled to the ground, spewing blood. In response to Quadehar's warning, some sorcerers quickly placed themselves under the protection of an Armor of Elhaz. But as Quadehar had foreseen, the frenzied monsters' attacks eventually broke down the feeble Galdrs that had been weakened by the countermagic of the talismans.

Despite the heroism of the sorcerers, who somehow managed to hold their own for a while, the expedition from The Lost Isle was slowly being decimated by the army of savage monsters.

With the help of a furiously projected Thursaz, Quadehar managed to rebuff the attack of a giant Hybrid. The creature fell to the ground, groaning. Beside him, protected by an Armor of Elhaz, which seemed to be holding out, two sorcerers cast spells on the enemy. In front of them, protected by the Naudhiz Stadha, three other comrades confronted the raging Orks. Quadehar's gaze swept the battlefield. Six! There were only six of them still on their feet out of the thirty who had left The Lost Isle! He clenched his fists. They had to find a refuge, at all costs.

"The tower!" he yelled to his fellow sorcerers. "Retreat to the tower!"

Moving out of range of the protection of their spells, the sorcerers raced after him. They reached the rickety beams that led to the top of the tower just moments ahead of the army of Orks.

"Oh no!" groaned Quadehar.

Stunned, the sorcerers could see that the beams nearest the ground had been sawed off to prevent access to the keep. Behind them, the monsters were closing in.

"We haven't got a moment to lose," said Ulriq, one of the surviving sorcerers. "You four — two of you take up the Naudhiz stance to protect the others, and two of you call up Thursaz! Get on with it and hold the Orks back as long as you can!"

Then he turned to Quadehar.

"I'll give you a leg up to the first beam. For the honor of The Lost Isle, you must get into this cursed tower and do battle with The Shadow."

Quadehar shook his head, "I'll never abandon you!"

Ulriq looked at him imploringly, "It's our only chance. The only chance of not dying for nothing. I beg you, Quadehar, you are the only one capable of doing it."

The Orks had now come up against the sorcerers' magic barrier, but the white glow of their pendants grew brighter. The protection wouldn't hold out for long. Ulriq braced himself against the wall of the tower and motioned to Quadehar.

The Master Sorcerer clambered resolutely onto his companion's shoulders. He grabbed the beam, then heaved himself up onto it. Ulriq shot him a parting look and then turned back to help the others.

Quadehar had tears in his eyes. At the foot of the tower, his friends were being massacred by the hordes from Yadigar who were protected by evil magic. The loathsome Thunku was going to pay dearly for this! But Ulriq was right — for the sacrifice of the sorcerers of the Guild not to be in vain, he had to find a way into this tower and face The Shadow, their ultimate enemy.

He closed his ears to the sorcerers' cries of agony and despair, and concentrated his mind on the fight ahead.

≋ ⁕ ≋ ⁕ ≋

Quadehar reached the platform at the top of the tower and immediately spotted a narrow door that was insecurely bolted. He projected the Uncertain Graphem of Elhaz, and that did the trick. The door opened, revealing a staircase leading down into the murky bowels of the building. Quadehar started his descent.

Lower down, he came across a metal door, which stood ajar. He pushed it open and entered a large, circular room whose walls were covered with bloodred hangings.

The place was in an indescribable state of chaos; everything was in turmoil. The furniture and tables had been overturned, books were strewn over the floor, and lying among them were broken alchemist's instruments. It looked as though the room had been searched from top to bottom.

In the center stood a Door, similar to the one that gave access from The Lost Isle to the Real and Uncertain Worlds. It was almost certainly the way Godfrey had reached the tower, only now it had been hacked to pieces.

Quadehar picked his way through the upturned furniture, the books, and the shattered instruments. He peered behind each hanging. Then he left the room and searched the rest of the tower.

It was deserted.

He made his way back up to the platform and, looking down on the battlefield and the raging ocean, he howled his fury to the winds.

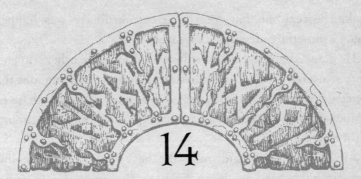

14

THE INTRUDER

Bertram decided to take Robin back to his room to try to comfort him. It was the most sensible thing to do, he thought. Sensible? Robin was certainly beginning to get to him! Bertram still didn't understand why his revelations about The Shadow had upset his friend so much. Did Robin know something about Lord Sha that nobody else did?

He offered to stay with him, but Robin refused with a wan smile of apology, assuring Bertram that he was fine but that he'd rather be on his own.

The young sorcerer left Robin in his room, and went downstairs to the courtyard at the heart of the monastery.

He walked across the empty space, under a cloudless sky, and entered the cloister. Suddenly, he heard a noise coming from the main door to the monastery . . . a violent thudding. He stopped.

At first he thought someone was banging on the outside to get in. But when the banging grew louder and the door began to shake, he realized that something extraordinary was happening . . . something deeply worrying.

He glanced around and saw he was alone. The other sorcerers were scattered around the monastery. Nobody had any idea that the center of sorcery of The Lost Isle was under attack at that very moment! Gifdu had never had a guard; the door alone was enough. Until now . . .

An extra violent thud made the heavy oak panels tremble. Bertram hid behind a column, his heart thumping. He feverishly felt for his sorcerer's bag, then he remembered that he'd left it in his room. He stifled a curse. Suddenly, with a terrifying creak, the door gave way and opened in a cloud of white smoke, out of which emerged a giant figure clad in a thick bloodred cloak.

The Shadow! He must be The Shadow, thought Bertram, regaining his composure. *Help! What am I going to do? Spirits of Gifdu, come to my aid!*

The man in red advanced with a heavy tread. He made a sign, and the door closed behind him with a loud bang.

"I must inform Charfalaq," Bertram said to himself. "If anyone is a match for The Shadow, he is! But how can I get word to him?"

While the junior sorcerer was wondering what to do, the intruder wove a Galdr against the door in a deep voice.

Then Bertram had a brainwave. "The bell! The big bell that's used to announce special visitors. If I ring it, the others will realize that something's happening! Come on, Bertram," he went on, steeling himself, "if you really are as good as you think you are, prove it! Be a credit to Gerald, and show him that he was right to make you a sorcerer, against everyone's advice."

Bertram took a deep breath and raced toward the wall where the chain that rang the heavy bronze bell hung. The man in red whirled around, but a fraction of a second too late. His freezing Graphem didn't begin to affect Bertram until after he had grabbed the chain.

The young sorcerer crumpled onto the ground as if he had received an electric shock, but the bell tolled urgently.

The man in red did not appear to panic. He took the time to invoke Perthro, the Guide, added Elhaz, which unlocks doors, Uruz, which pacifies the spirits of a place, and Isaz, which helps concentration, then whispered Robin's name onto the Lokk he had created. . . . He let the spell take effect, then set off down the corridors of the monastery knowing exactly where to go.

≋　✳　≋　✳　≋

The clanging of the great bell broke into Robin's thoughts. Who could the unusual visitor be? He ambled lazily over to the window and looked out into the courtyard. He froze. From where he stood, he could see Bertram lying unconscious near the main door, and beside him, the massive silhouette of a man wearing a bloodred cloak.

Robin leaped back from the window. Oh no! Who was it? Surely not The Shadow? Whoever it was, it was someone who had managed to break down Gifdu's defenses and overpower a sorcerer!

Robin went back to the window and studied the intruder more closely. He couldn't hear him, of course, but by watching his fingers as he formed Mudra and drew Graphems in the air, he knew that he was composing a spell.

"Perthro, Elhaz, Uruz, Isaz . . ." murmured Robin to himself. "Galdr or Lokk, this fellow is creating a magical compass that will overcome any obstacle! He's looking for someone, that's for sure. And I fear it might be *me* he's after! In any case, it's not a good idea to stay here."

Robin grabbed his bag and, as the intruder entered the main building before him, he headed down the other staircase leading to the courtyard.

Once in the cloister, he raced over to the main door, stopping briefly to check that Bertram was still breathing, then tried to open it — in vain. The door was sealed from the inside.

Robin's mind was racing. His only chance of escape was to vanish into the labyrinth of corridors below ground level and lie low. . . .

He wasted no more time and disappeared down a corridor.

≈ ✳ ≈ ✳ ≈

Just as Robin left the courtyard, the man in red entered the room he'd left a few moments earlier. A quick glance informed him that Robin was no longer there. The Lokk prompted him not to waste any more time and led him back down to the ground floor.

At an intersection, he came face to face with a small group of sorcerers heading for the main entrance, with Qadwan and Gerald at their head. With astonishing speed, he cast a freezing spell, which riveted the poor souls to the floor.

Then, without paying further heed to the sorcerers who were angrily gesticulating and shouting, he set off into the labyrinth below. He hesitated at the first intersection, and turned right. The corridor seemed to lead down to the basement. At the second intersection, he consulted a Talking Stone and received the confirmation that he was indeed descending into the bowels of Gifdu.

15

CAT AND MOUSE

Robin tore down the corridors, making his way into the very depths of the monastery.

He delved into his bag and fished out his well-thumbed map of the site. He'd printed it out when he'd hacked into the monastery's computer during his previous stay there, three months earlier. He feverishly checked the map whenever he was in doubt as to where he was or which way to go. The patches of phosphorescent lichen on the walls and ceilings gave out a feeble glow.

The Talking Stones also confirmed his whereabouts and helped him decide his direction. Some of them hadn't been touched for a long time and before he could decipher them he had to wipe off a layer of dust. He tried to take as many detours as possible to throw his pursuer off the scent.

From time to time, he heard footsteps echoing in a distant corridor. It must be the man in the red cloak getting closer!

Deep down inside, he knew it would be difficult to keep his pursuer at bay. In the courtyard, he had seen the intruder form an orientation and search spell, which was probably aimed at him! He had to keep a distance between himself and the man in red at all costs, and hope that he would eventually tire, or that the spell would go awry.

Robin soon found himself at a major intersection. He paused and consulted the map: The corridor on the left went directly up to the ground-floor level, the one facing him led to a dead end, and the one on the right led to a disused mine. Now was the time to try and throw off his pursuer!

He stopped for a moment to reflect on the best strategy. He was amazed that he was able to stay so calm when this game of cat and mouse might be a matter of life and death for him! But he was always at his best under pressure. Perhaps because action was the only thing that mattered, and action stopped you from having to think about more difficult problems.

He began by taking out of his bag the fake Talking Stone that had once gotten him into trouble and cost him his dessert. Today, it might help save his life.

He moistened the arrows with his spit and reshaped the papier-mâché stone, then blew on it to harden it again. He hung up the fake stone, which now showed a second dead end instead of the corridor leading to the disused mine.

Then he set off down the left-hand corridor, which led to the surface. After a short distance, he retraced his steps back to the intersection.

There, he invoked Dagaz, the Graphem that made time stand still and gave you mental invisibility when formulated differently, and stabilized it with a Mudra.

Then he set off down the right-hand corridor that led to the mine.

≈ ✳ ≈ ✳ ≈

Shortly afterward, the man in red paused at the intersection. The power of the investigative Lokk was beginning to wear off. It did, however, clearly indicate that his quarry had taken the corridor on the left. He consulted the Talking Stone: That corridor led up to the surface. The young apprentice probably hadn't hesitated for long. . . .

The man stopped to check where the other corridors led: two dead ends. He wasted no more time and was soon pounding along the corridor that led up to the surface.

≈ ✳ ≈ ✳ ≈

Soon, Robin could no longer hear footsteps behind him. His trick had worked! He sank down on the floor of one of the rooms, probably an old warehouse in the days when the mine was working.

Now that the hunt was over, he was trembling from head to foot. Instinctively, he fumbled beneath his sweater for the sun-shaped pendant that his father had left for him before disappearing. Robin had never taken it off before Agatha had snatched it, and that had led to her being kidnapped in his place by the Gommons. But then he remembered — stupid him! The pendant was no longer there. Agatha hadn't been able to return it to him because one of Thunku's soldiers had stolen it from her upon her arrival in The Uncertain World. Robin desperately needed something to cling to right now, even if it was only a token from an unknown father.

It took him a moment to calm down. He etched Dagaz in the earth with his Ristir, so that the Graphem would retain its power. Then he took from his bag the supplies he always caried — a little bottle of water and two apples. All he had to do now was wait.

16
ROBIN DISPLAYS HIS SKILL

Robin munched on half an apple and drank a mouthful of water. Then he settled himself comfortably and took from his bag a long, soft, light-gray garment, a Little Man of Virdu cloak, which he had stolen from the monastery last summer and worn all the time during his escapade in The Uncertain World. He always kept it with him. He wrapped himself up in its comforting folds and, tired from his frightening ordeal, allowed himself to drift off to sleep.

He had a strange dream. Master Quadehar was banging on the door of the monastery shouting: "Robin! Robin! Open the door!"

He awoke with a start. The image of Quadehar had vanished, but he could still distinctly hear his voice! He clutched his head.

"Robin, can you hear me?"

"Master! Is it you?" stammered Robin in amazement.

"Yes, it's me, but there's no point in shouting, I'm speaking to you inside your head. Answer me in the same way."

"But . . . how is it possible?"

"I wove a spell using Berkana, the Graphem that makes it possible to enter into communication with the spirits. I had difficulty finding you. . . ."

"It's because I engraved Dagaz beside me . . . but what are you doing here?"

"We were ambushed in The Uncertain World. I haven't got time to explain. For heaven's sake, Robin, tell me what's going on! I'm outside the monastery and the door won't open. Nobody's answering my shouts!"

"It's The Shadow, Master," explained Robin, forming the words in his mind. "A very tall man with a huge red cloak. He managed to open the door and knock Bertram out . . . and maybe all the sorcerers, too. I saw him weaving a search spell. I think he's after me, Master!"

"Calm down, Robin. Where are you?"

"I'm underground, in a corridor leading to the disused mine. I think I've managed to throw him off."

"Be very careful, Robin. Whether he's The Shadow or not, this man sounds like a very powerful magician."

"You've got to help me, Master. . . . Do something!"

"The door is blocked from the inside, and the spells cast by the Guild around Gifdu prevent me from using the paths of the Wyrd to reach you. I'll see what I can do, but it looks . . . watch out, Robin! Somebody's trying to intercept our conversation! I'm going to have to switch the Berkana spell off to prevent them from finding you. . . ."

Quadehar's voice faded and Robin found himself alone again. But he knew that his master was there, ready to come to his rescue, and that cheered him up. However, his mysterious pursuer, briefly thrown off the scent, was clearly on to him again.

Perhaps he didn't have as much time as he thought!

"Think Robin, think!" he urged himself.

He must, at all costs, unblock the wretched main door, and put himself out of reach of the man in the red cloak, at least until his master came to his aid. The second problem seemed the easiest to resolve first and he put his mind to it. He started thinking aloud, trying to organize his mind:

"I must be prepared for the arrival of the man in red . . . but how do I put myself out of danger? The other night, Master Quadehar talked about the Armor of Elhaz Galdr and the Helmet of Terror Lokk. He said that one of them was more reliable and that the other was more powerful. Which one should I choose? Admittedly, I'm better at Galdrs. But will that be strong enough against this man? Let's see . . . he's managed to get inside Gifdu. I'm afraid that even the Helmet Lokk won't be powerful enough to stop him! And suppose . . . suppose I tried something else? But what if I fail?"

He moved to the center of the room, grasped his dagger, and drew six symbols around him, as he had seen his master do in front of the sorcerers in the training room. But it wasn't Elhaz that he fixed on the ground! He tried to reproduce, six times in a row, and as precisely as possible, the Helmet of Terror Lokk that his master had drawn in the air while he'd watched from his hiding place the night before.

"I'm taking a big risk," he said to himself. "Master Quadehar said so: one mistake and the whole Lokk fails. I did six! Six more chances that it will all backfire!"

His job done, Robin rested for a moment. He was sweating from the effort of concentration and he felt exhausted. Then he uttered the incantation of the Armor Galdr, changing it slightly:

"By the power of Elhaz, Erda, and Kari, Rind, Hir, and Loge, Egishjamur in front, Egishjamur behind, Egishjamur to the left, Egishjamur to the right, Egishjamur above, and Egishjamur below, Egishjamur protect me! ALU!"

He had combined the power of a Lokk and a Galdr. Would that succeed in stopping his pursuer? Robin felt the air tremble around him. Then everything went back to normal.

"Please let it work," he breathed.

Now he had to deal with the door. But how, he wondered. How could he open it from his underground hideout? His knowledge was certainly not powerful enough to create a spell at a distance. And the man in red was bound to have covered the door with protective Graphems! He'd have to think of another indirect way, one that hadn't occurred to his pursuer.

Robin had a sudden realization. He rummaged around in his bag and found his notebook. He took out a sheet of paper folded in four — the printout of the directory list of files stored on Gifdu's computer, which he'd "borrowed" from the computer at the same time as the map of the monastery. He scanned it excitedly.

"Menus for November, Budget for the current year, List of those hostile to the Guild . . . Ah, here we are: Monastery security! I'm sure I'll find a solution to opening the door in there. Only . . . only I'm in the farthest place from the computer room, and I don't have a laptop in my bag!"

The sound of his own voice reassured him, but his mind was

racing. Without thinking, he tapped the ground, and suddenly he stiffened. That was it! He'd found the solution! He didn't have a computer, so he'd just have to improvise one!

He picked up his Ristir dagger again and drew the shape of a computer screen and keyboard on the ground, as accurately as he could. That was the easy bit. Then he took a few moments to think, and decided to create a Galdr by calling up Fehu, which imbued objects with energy, and Gebu, which established communication:

"*By the power of Frey and the Spider, of Gefn and the Gift, Fehu raised with the Wolf, Gebu the haven of the poor, sleeping and waking, I call on your energies! FEG!*"

The computer screen that Robin had drawn on the ground glowed feebly. He leaned over and, to his relief, saw the cursor flickering in the top left-hand corner. He couldn't see much, but it would do!

Carefully pressing the keys of the dirt keyboard, he typed in "The Master of the Keep," the password that had already given him access to the secret program. He could barely recognize the home page, the glow from the screen was so pale. He managed to make out "Password," flashing against a starry background.

He cast the same spell as before, drawing Elhaz and making the Graphem crack the electronic code. He soon found himself in the forbidden menu. He went straight to the *Monastery security* file and hit the Return key.

There was a little mud on his fingertip; this felt so strange!

"Let's see . . . let's look under *In an emergency*."

The Return key, which had been slightly smudged, did not

respond so well. Robin then discovered, under the sub-heading *Main door*, a file called *An improvement by Gerald*. He opened it immediately.

"Great!" exulted Robin. "You can open the door from the computer! It's linked to a mechanical opening system. . . . Gerald must have been fed up with the others making fun of his computer knowledge. And I bet he hasn't told a soul!"

Robin clicked on the icon *Control the emergency mechanism for opening the door*.

Nothing happened.

"Oh, it's too stupid!" he moaned.

Then he realized that the Return key was almost entirely obliterated. He picked up his Ristir and redrew it, then pressed it again. This time, the computer registered the command. He wasn't able to check whether, above ground, the mechanism activating the door was going to prove more powerful than the spells of the man in red. But he desperately hoped so!

In front of him, the screen of the makeshift computer flickered, then faded. Robin brushed his hand over it and kept on waiting.

17

A SURPRISE REUNION

The sound of heavy, plodding footsteps made Robin jump. Somebody was approaching his hiding place!

Without panicking, he checked that the Lokk surrounding him, which he had woven into a protective Galdr, was still in place.

A shape loomed at the end of the stone passageway. Robin's heart thumped at the sight of the massive silhouette shrouded in a bloodred cloak. When the man spotted Robin, he stopped. He removed his hood to reveal his face, which was half-hidden by several days' stubble.

He had brown, curly hair and beautiful eyes the color of amethysts. He wasn't very old — around thirty or thirty-five perhaps.

He spoke to Robin in a deep voice.

"Well, you've certainly led me a fine dance! Very clever, the fake Talking Stone. And I bet you've concealed your mental identity behind good old Dagaz! Am I right?"

"Who are you?" asked Robin, disconcerted by his pursuer's appearance and friendly tone.

"Where I come from, they call me Lord Sha."

"Lo . . . Lord Sha?" stuttered Robin.

"You've heard of me?" asked the man in red, taken aback.

"Let's say . . . there are stories about you. . . ."

"Stories that are far removed from the truth, believe me," broke in Lord Sha. "My story will perhaps find its ending here. . . . Don't be afraid. I'm not going to hurt you."

He moved forward. Instinctively, Robin recoiled, then he remembered that he was protected by a Galdr and raised his head in defiance. He hoped fervently that his spell would be powerful enough to hold out.

Within inches of Robin, the man came up against an invisible wall where the Egishjamur had been drawn. He murmured in surprise, then stepped back a few paces and made a complicated gesture in the air. There was a shower of golden sparks.

The protection of the Armor of Elhaz, constructed by Robin and reinforced by the power of a Lokk, faltered but held strong. Lord Sha let out a whistle of admiration.

"Bravo! I don't know if I could have done better myself!"

He looked at the boy with amusement. Robin returned his gaze without flinching.

"I suppose there's no point asking you to lower your defenses. Understandably, you're afraid of me. I could, of course, break down your protection, given a bit of time, but I'm not trying to catch you. I just want to know something. And a simple spell will suffice for that."

The man drew a new series of Graphems in the air and muttered some strange words. Robin immediately began to feel an odd sensation.

It felt as though there was something creeping around inside his head, visiting his brain. Robin moaned. He wished he could resist this unpleasant intrusion and drive away the invisible fingers nimbly rummaging around in his mind.

He tried to summon the Graphems to his assistance, but none of them replied. Then the icy sensation stopped as suddenly as it had started. From the other side of the Armor of Elhaz, Lord Sha was gazing at him in disappointment.

"I'm so sorry. I'd been told . . . I thought that . . . but you're not the boy I hoped to find. Unfortunately . . . I hope you'll forgive me for having frightened you."

Just as Lord Sha uttered these baffling words, there was a deafening explosion and Quadehar burst into the room.

"Robin!" he cried on discovering his apprentice sitting in the center of an Armor of Elhaz, confronting a terrifying form. "Are you all right?"

"Fine, Master! Am I glad to see you!"

"Likewise, my boy!"

Quadehar turned to the cloaked intruder who hadn't moved.

"Whoever you are, you're going to be sorry you ever entered Gifdu and threatened my pupil," he warned.

The sorcerer adopted an aggressive Stadha and faced his opponent. But when he caught sight of Lord Sha's face, he froze in amazement.

"You? I thought you were dead! Where have you been hiding? What are you doing here?"

"Yes, it's me, old friend!" replied the man with a rueful smile. "As for the rest, you'll have to find out the answer for yourself. . . ."

Taking advantage of Quadehar's surprise, Lord Sha leaped

forward and floored the sorcerer with a well-aimed punch, then fled off down the corridor.

Robin hurriedly erased the protective spell with his foot and went to help his master, who lay stunned on the floor.

Robin propped Quadehar up against the wall in a sitting position and gave him the rest of his water to drink.

"Are you okay, Master?"

"Yes, Robin. Thank you. If I hadn't been exhausted by all this traveling between the Worlds, I'd never have allowed myself to be caught off guard."

"Shouldn't we go after him?"

Wearily, Quadehar gave a dismissive wave.

"No point. He's probably already left The Lost Isle by now."

"Did you see Bertram? He was lying unconscious near the entrance. Has he come around?"

"Your friend regained consciousness when the door . . . by the way, how did you manage to open it? And what were you doing sitting there surrounded by an Armor of Elhaz?"

"I'll tell you all about it later, Master," replied Robin evasively, going red. "Do you know if Gerald and the others are OK?"

"Yes, they're safe and sound, battling against a freezing spell. Except Charfalaq, who kept out of the way. In any case, shut away in his tower, he wouldn't even know if The Lost Isle sank into the sea! I didn't have time to release him, I was in too much of a hurry to find you."

"So, Lord Sha isn't evil because he didn't actually kill anyone!"

"Lord Sha? How do you know that's Lord Sha?" spluttered Quadehar.

"He told me so, Master. Besides, he didn't seem to have any harmful intentions toward me. He was simply trying to find something out. And I get the feeling he was disappointed. . . ."

"Lord Sha," echoed Quadehar, suddenly pensive. "We've been on the wrong track from the start. Dear me, none of this makes any sense!"

"What happened in The Uncertain World, Master?"

Quadehar leaned against the wall and sighed deeply.

"They were expecting us. We were ambushed. We were attacked by hundreds of Orks. While my band of sorcerers was being set upon, I broke into Lord Sha's tower, where we thought The Shadow was hiding. But the place was deserted. Meanwhile, Sha was breaking down the door of Gifdu. . . ."

"Where he, too, thought he'd find the person he was looking for," Robin went on. "But somebody other than me! Who that is, I have no idea."

"What do you mean? That you're not the person he's looking for? Are you sure?" asked Quadehar, watching Robin out of the corner of his eye.

"That's what he told me. Does that surprise you, Master?"

"No, no . . ." replied Quadehar vaguely. "Clearly everyone was expecting to find someone else," he added, perplexed.

"What do you mean? Oh, Master . . . please, answer me! After what happened today, I have a right to know!"

"Calm down, Robin. Yes, you do have a right to know. What I mean is that we attacked Jaghatel because we thought that Lord Sha and The Shadow were one and the same person. But Sha can't be The Shadow. . . ."

"How do you know?"

"Because the man who told you his name is Sha is actually Yorwan, a former student who was in the year below me at Gifdu. He's the brilliant and promising sorcerer who vanished one day, taking the *Book of the Stars* with him. Nobody has ever been able to track him down in The Uncertain World. We all believed he was dead. . . ."

≈ ✳ ≈ ✳ ≈

Lord Sha emerged near his tower, in the ruins of Jaghatel. Once outside Gifdu, he had used the Desert Galdr to get home.

As he had torn along the corridors of the monastery, which brought back painful memories with every step, he told himself that he had been lucky to get the better of Quadehar so easily. His former fellow student seemed to have developed his skills to an impressive level: To break the spells he'd placed on the door of Gifdu required extraordinary magic powers. It had been a good idea to use his fists against the sorcerer rather than Graphems!

As he made his way toward his tower, he thought about the boy who radiated an astonishing force, and who might so easily have been . . . He was overwhelmed by a profound sense of disappointment.

Nearing the door to the Tower of Jaghatel, he came across the first of the dead Orks and the bodies of sorcerers still enveloped in their unmistakable dark cloaks. He cried out in astonishment.

"What's happened?"

Then he opened the door and ran up the stairs of the tower.

He pushed open the metal door of his laboratory and stopped dead, transfixed by the sight that greeted him. The entire room had been ransacked. He swore, strode over to the red hangings and ripped them from the walls, uttering an opening spell. A section of the wall slid aside to reveal a cupboard. It was empty.

"We are lost!" wailed Yorwan, sinking to his knees.

18

AN UNEXPECTED VISIT

Robin opened the door of the house where he lived with his mother, on the edge of the village of Penmarch, and rushed into the kitchen. He put the loaf of bread he'd just bought from the baker on the table, then raced up the stairs to his room.

He flung himself onto the bed and took from his apprentice's bag the comic book he'd bought in the village store, a shop that sold absolutely everything, from sweets to newspapers to computer parts. He flipped through the pages, lingered over some of the new characters, then began reading.

"Robin! You didn't forget the bread, did you?"

"No, Mom! I put it in the kitchen!"

"Thank you, darling!"

He heard his mother moving around downstairs, and felt an immense sense of relief. The cupboard doors opening and closing, the clinking of the glasses as she put them away, the sound of water running as she turned on the tap . . . it reminded him of the normal pattern of his everyday life before all *this* happened.

Robin stopped reading and stretched out on his back, his hands behind his head. His world was quite small when he thought about it: his home, his mother, school, Agatha and Thomas, the heath and Gifdu, Master Quadehar . . . not forgetting, of course, Amber, Coral, Godfrey, and Romaric! Not everybody was lucky enough to have such wonderful friends!

Last summer, on their return from their unbelievable adventures in The Uncertain World, the Provost had held a big party in their honor. Robin and Amber had danced for hours by the fire, and that had been really fun. Except at the end, when he'd found her looking at him in that very strange way. . . .

Godfrey had come to introduce his newfound friend, a pretty, auburn-haired girl from the village of Atteti, in the Golden Mountains. Later, they'd joined Coral and Romaric at a table for a glass of apple cider. His cousin was blushing, and Coral was more cheerful than usual.

Robin bit his lip: Was something more than friendship blossoming between them?

The apprentice sorcerer couldn't help envying their carefree air. Now, he was preoccupied with questions to which he had no answer. His encounter with Lord Sha, about which he hadn't breathed a word to his friends, preyed on his mind. Agatha had told him that Sha was seeking the son who had been stolen from him; a son who would now be about twelve years old. Then the man in red had said, *"You're not the boy I hoped to find."*

What did it all mean? That the attempts to kidnap him had nothing to do with his gift for magic? That it wasn't The Shadow who was behind all this scheming, but Lord Sha? Convinced that Robin was his son, had he been trying to get him back? How could Robin find out . . . and what was the connection with the *Book of the Stars*, that Sha/Yorwan had stolen when he was young?

These thoughts were going around and around in Robin's mind, making him feel dizzy. Did somebody have the answer? Did somebody know the truth?

One thing at least was certain: Without being able to explain it, Robin felt sad. Sad, perhaps, that he was not Sha's long-lost son. Sad to be fatherless . . .

He sighed, then picked up his comic book again in an attempt to distract himself.

≈ ✳ ≈ ✳ ≈

A few minutes later, when he was happily absorbed in the story, his mother called up the stairs, "Robin, you have a visitor!"

Robin hated being interrupted when he was reading. He raised himself up on his elbows and asked irritably, "Who is it?"

"It's a school friend! Shall I send her up?"

A girl from school? Robin racked his brains. No, he had no idea who might come and visit him in Penmarch. Intrigued, he called down, "Yes, thanks" and sat up on the bed.

Somebody climbed the stairs with a light step, hesitated in front of the door, on which Robin had stuck a poster saying "DO NOT DISTURB: POWERFUL SORCERER BATTLING AGAINST EVIL FORCES," then knocked.

"Come in!"

A familiar figure slid into his room and closed the door behind her. Robin's heart missed a beat.

"Hi, Robin! How are you?"

It was Agatha! Agatha Balangru . . .

"Er . . . fine, thanks," stammered Robin, at a loss. What was *she* doing here?

"I told your mother that I was your classmate," explained the tall girl, walking over to him. "What are you reading?"

"A comic book . . . with sorcerers, knights, and trolls. It's good. . . ."

Agatha made herself at home and, sitting down on the bed with incredible assurance, began flicking casually through the comic. Robin felt his cheeks burning. . . .

He couldn't believe his eyes! He secretly pinched himself: No, he wasn't dreaming! His ex-worst enemy was there, in his house, in his room, on his bed, reading his comic book! He shuddered at the thought of Amber walking in right then. It was almost better when Agatha used to bully him.

"Ahem . . ." Robin began awkwardly. "Wh . . . where's Thomas? Isn't he with you?"

"No," she replied, gazing at Robin with her half-closed eyes. "His father needed him. I took advantage of being on my own to come and see you."

"Oh, right. Er . . . why?"

"Can't you guess?"

Robin's mouth suddenly felt dry, and he had difficulty swallowing.

"N . . . no."

"To invite you to the Samain party, of course! My father's letting me use his house. There'll just be Thomas and me."

Robin stifled a huge sigh of relief. What an idiot he was! For a terrifying moment, he had thought she was going to kiss him!

He steadied his nerves and carefully replied, "That's really nice of you, Agatha, but . . . I've already got plans to spend Samain with Romaric, Godfrey, and the twins. Amber and Coral's father's lending us his apartment."

"Pity," sighed Agatha, shaking her dark hair, which she'd been growing longer. "But I'm not really surprised. The five of you are inseparable! Anyway," she added, getting to her feet, "we're bound to bump into each other. The celebrations last for three days, and Dashtikazar isn't very big!"

"Yes, I'm sure we'll bump into each other," echoed Robin, desperately hoping they wouldn't. Amber would probably find it hard to understand the new relationship Agatha was trying to build with him. . . .

"Right. I must be off. It's quite a trek you know, to get out here!"

Before Robin could respond, Agatha leaned over and kissed him on the cheek. Then she vanished. Robin sat there dazed. Again, he hoped with all his heart that they wouldn't bump into each other during the Samain holidays!

19

A MEETING OF THE GUILD

"Quadehar, it's time."

Two sorcerers, whose names escaped him, had come to fetch the master from the room where he was being kept prisoner. Quadehar sighed and rose from the chair where he'd been meditating for too many long hours.

"I am ready."

He stepped into the corridor. His new jailers led him toward the gymnasium. When he entered the vast room, the buzz of conversation ceased, and countless pairs of eyes turned to stare at him. Makeshift seating had been erected, and some hundred and fifty men wearing the dark cloaks of the Guild were sitting there.

They're closing ranks, thought Quadehar with a wry smile.

His guards led him to the center of the room. Opposite him, on a platform, sat a tribunal of five sorcerers.

Quadehar recognized the man who was acting as public prosecutor in this absurd trial: He was the Chief Sorcerer of the Monastery of Gri, an establishment of the Guild that stood on the far side of the Dark Moor. Quadehar did not like this wizened, embittered old man. Unfortunately, the feeling was mutual. He had disliked Quadehar since the day when the sorcerer had made fun of a book about telling the future from fish entrails in front of its author, the Chief Sorcerer of Gri.

The four other members of the Council were Charfalaq, who seemed to be half-dead as usual; Gerald, who looked glum; and two middle-aged, middle-ranking sorcerers whom he vaguely remembered from Dashtikazar or elsewhere.

The Chief Sorcerer of Gri rose and addressed him.

"Quadehar, brother sorcerer. The Guild has called this Council to investigate the tragic massacre of Jaghatel. We await your explanation."

Quadehar began to speak, his voice calm but loud enough to be heard by the entire assembly.

"This charade is ridiculous! I have already given a detailed report. As I have told you, we walked into an ambush set up by Thunku and his Orks from Yadigar aided by a powerful magician. Powerful enough to protect the monsters from the Guild's spells. I don't think Thunku is the brains behind the operation. He was probably working for someone else. . . . However, I repeat, they were waiting for us at Jaghatel!"

"Don't you have anything more convincing to say?" broke in the Chief Sorcerer of Gri, impatiently.

"Now look," went on Quadehar, beginning to get really angry, "I saw sorcerers, many of whom were friends, die at Jaghatel! What more do you want?"

"You see, Quadehar," continued the Chief Sorcerer of Gri,

narrowing his eyes, "what we find so odd is that you are the only one to have survived this dreadful attack unharmed. . . ."

Indignant murmurs swept through the room, and there was an outburst of support for Quadehar.

"What are you daring to insinuate?" thundered the Master Sorcerer. "That I enjoyed watching my friends being massacred in front of my eyes?"

Gerald then rose to his feet and, speaking in a slightly trembling voice, prevented the Chief Sorcerer of Gri from attacking Quadehar again.

"Let us allow Quadehar to tell us more about what happened!"

The gathering noisily agreed and the Chief Sorcerer had no choice but to back down, with obvious bad grace. Quadehar calmed himself, and spoke once again in a clear voice.

"Thank you, Gerald. Our objective in going to The Uncertain World was to vanquish The Shadow. When we realized that the battle with the Orks was hopeless, we decided that we had to make one last attempt to attack our enemy in his tower. My companions insisted I should be the one to do so. Unfortunately, the tower was deserted and, on my return, I found the sorcerers had all been slaughtered. . . ."

"Alone? Why did you go into the tower alone?" challenged the Chief Sorcerer of Gri.

"Because the others were either dead or locked in combat with the Orks and, in the end, because I'm the only person capable of taking on The Shadow. . . ."

"What arrogance!" exclaimed the Chief Sorcerer of Gri, falling silent when Charfalaq raised his hand to speak.

"Quadehar," croaked the Grand Master of the Guild, before being overcome by a terrible fit of coughing, "is indeed the Guild's most able sorcerer. . . ."

"Thank you for confirming that, Master," replied the Chief Sorcerer of Gri in syrupy tones, bowing ingratiatingly. "But that," he snapped, turning toward Quadehar, "still does not explain why you are the only survivor."

The Chief Sorcerer of Gri then addressed the assembled sorcerers, who were now feeling uneasy, "Isn't it rather strange that our brother sorcerer should be the only one to come out alive? Isn't it also strange that they were expecting our expedition at Jaghatel when it was planned with the utmost secrecy? I think we were betrayed! And that the traitor is here! Standing before us! I suggest he should be neutralized by a collective spell and locked up in one of the dungeons at Gri!"

The closing speech for the prosecution led to a furor. The sorcerers rose from their seats, and many shouted that it was all slander and lies. The Chief Sorcerer of Gri called out: "To the dungeon!" pointing theatrically at Quadehar, who decided to wait until calm was restored. Charfalaq seemed completely out of his depth. It was Gerald who finally obtained silence by banging the table several times.

"Calm down everyone, please! Quiet! And let us be reasonable! The dungeon . . . Why not to the torture chamber, or the stake, while we're at it?"

The assembly seemed relieved at his mocking words, whereas the Chief Sorcerer of Gri glared daggers at him.

"To take a more reasonable approach, I suggest that a special Commission be appointed to carry out a thorough investigation into the tragedy of Jaghatel. In the meantime, Quadehar will remain confined at Gifdu and will be banned from leaving. What is the Council's view?"

Charfalaq, on whom all eyes had converged, seemed to have fallen asleep.

"I'm against!" thundered the Chief Sorcerer of Gri.

"Is anybody else against?" went on Gerald, looking the other two sorcerers straight in the eyes. They bowed their heads. "Nobody? Good, then the Council therefore accepts my suggestion. The hearing is over!"

Furious, the Chief Sorcerer of Gri stepped down from the platform and marched out of the gymnasium, taking with him his entourage who had accompanied him from the Dark Moor.

Quadehar was released. But nobody would look him in the eye as they left. Only Gerald winked at him as he walked past.

20
WORDS OF WISDOM

Standing in the little cell in the heart of the monastery, Quadehar was overwhelmed by a mass of contradictory feelings. How had things come to this?

A few days earlier, he had been chosen to lead the boldest attack ever launched by the Guild against The Shadow; at that point, he had been considered the most able and powerful sorcerer of The Lost Isle, and it was generally thought that he was the natural successor to Charfalaq. Strange irony! And now, stripped of his rights and the object of general suspicion, he was being held prisoner at Gifdu, pending the findings of a dubious Commission of Inquiry.

Of course, he could come and go freely within the monastery, but he was not allowed to leave the premises, and he knew that he was being discreetly spied on; every move he made was being watched.

Quadehar clenched his fists in anger. He felt wounded by the attitude of his fellow sorcerers.

When he had explained what had really happened at the Tower of Jaghatel to the Council, nobody had appeared to believe him, apart from Gerald, who had defended him. Charfalaq, the Chief Sorcerer, had been content merely to reaffirm his esteem for Quadehar, but had done nothing to help him out of this tight spot. As for the Chief Sorcerer of Gri's argument, it was very simple and even made sense. Given that the expedition had been planned in the utmost secrecy, how had it come about that the sorcerers were expected at Jaghatel? That was what really upset Quadehar, that his fellow sorcerers could doubt his word.

But there was something that troubled him much more than his own hurt feelings. The Chief Sorcerer of Gri was right: Nobody, apart from the Guild, had known about the attack plan. Which meant that somebody inside the Guild had passed on information to Thunku! So there was a traitor in their midst. A traitor who was perhaps working for The Shadow.

Quadehar shuddered at the thought.

What did Gerald think? He shook himself, left the room, and headed toward the computer room where he was bound to find the computer wizard.

≈ ✳ ≈ ✳ ≈

As Quadehar wandered through the corridors, he thought about the other incident that had perturbed him deeply. Yorwan! He was well and truly alive, and perfectly at home, so it seemed, in the guise of Lord Sha!

When he had set off to track down Yorwan in The Uncertain World, after the theft of the *Book of the Stars* all those years ago, Quadehar had searched high and low and carried out a long and painstaking investigation that had brought him to the conclusion that Yorwan must be dead. He had vanished, and everybody was convinced that he'd been killed by brigands who had robbed him, and then disposed of his body.

Years later, when Lord Sha had appeared at Jaghatel, reports from Pursuers had described a gifted but ruthless magician from Ferghana who had a fearsome reputation in The Uncertain World. After that, Lord Sha had lain low, and the Pursuers had left it at that.

Who could have imagined that Lord Sha and Yorwan were one and the same person? Quadehar recalled his surprise on recognizing his former fellow student as the man who was stalking Robin. The whole business seemed very complicated: What was the meaning of the mysterious words Yorwan had uttered to Robin before fleeing? And could Yorwan in some way have been involved in the Jaghatel massacre? And what was his relationship to The Shadow?

He turned these questions over and over in his mind, but was unable to find any answers. One thing was certain, however: The Shadow, Sha, the *Book of the Stars* — as Charfalaq had always supposed — were all connected to Robin! Why? He'd find out in the end. To the devil with the Commission investigating the massacre, to the devil with the Guild and the Chief Sorcerer! The truth was elsewhere, and he was going to uncover it. . . .

≈ ✳ ≈ ✳ ≈

Quadehar walked into the big room housing the computers that Gerald maintained for the use of Gifdu's guests. The sorcerer was in his office, by the door. Beside him sat a haughty-looking young man who was helping him with some filing.

"What a pleasant surprise!" exclaimed Gerald on seeing Quadehar. "I thought you were going on a hunger strike in your cell!"

Short, potbellied, and bespectacled, with a mischievous twinkle in his eyes, Gerald was known — and feared — for his sharp sense of humor. His almost bald head was home to one of the Guild's most brilliant minds. Even if he wasn't as adept as others at manipulating the Graphems and was often teased by the younger sorcerers, he was brilliant at solving problems and his advice was often sought by the wisest of his colleagues. That is why he was able to sway the Council, and save Quadehar from the dungeons of Gri.

Quadehar jerked his chin inquiringly in the direction of the young man who stared at him nonchalantly.

"Don't worry, my old friend," Gerald reassured him. "Let me introduce Bertram, a newly ordained sorcerer, who was my apprentice. I have every faith in him."

"Bertram, of course!" nodded Quadehar. "I'm sorry, I didn't recognize you — last time I saw you, you were lying in a heap by the monastery door!"

Bertram was about to reply with his customary impudence, but Gerald restrained him, laughing.

"Don't tease him too much. He's really very shy."

"I'm used to it," replied Quadehar. "I have an apprentice who turns as red as a beetroot at the slightest provocation!"

"That doesn't surprise me," retorted Gerald, "given that you're such a monster, or so the Guild would have us believe!"

Quadehar became serious again.

"How many people still consider me a sorcerer worthy of the name?"

"It's hard to say. As far as Qadwan and I are concerned, there's no doubt, but sadly the same doesn't go for some of the others . . . second-rate sorcerers. Charfalaq respects you, there's no doubt about that either, but it's increasingly difficult to tell what the old fellow thinks. . . ."

"As far as I'm concerned, the Chief Sorcerer of Gri's hatred toward you is enough to make me take your side!" cut in Bertram.

"Thank you, Bertram," replied Quadehar, taken aback. "I share your feelings . . ." he turned to Gerald, "but maybe this young sorcerer should learn to keep his opinions to himself!"

"He hasn't ever let me down," said Gerald defensively. "Well, not really!"

"I've thought long and hard," went on Quadehar, becoming serious again. "I believe there's a traitor within the Guild."

Bertram raised an eyebrow, but his former master did not seem surprised.

"I have reached the same conclusion myself."

"In your opinion, what should I do?"

Gerald looked Quadehar straight in the eye and declared, "This whole business doesn't make sense. Somebody must get to the bottom of things. Qadwan's getting old. As for me, with Charfalaq going senile, I've got to keep an eye on Gifdu. Quadehar, my friend, you're the only one who can do it!"

"So you advise me to . . ."

". . . get out of here and conduct your own investigation,

in absolute freedom. Why do you think I suggested the idea of that ridiculous Commission? To gain time. So make the most of it. . . ."

Quadehar thought for a moment, weighing the pros and the cons.

"Yes, it's a possibility. I know a place where I could stay. There's somebody who has no great liking for the Guild who will welcome me with open arms. But the problem is that my investigation will take me back into The Uncertain World."

"So?" queried Gerald.

"Robin will be left alone on The Lost Isle, with nobody to protect him. That's a real worry now. Especially as I can't even risk leaving him at Gifdu with a traitor lurking under the same roof!"

At the mere mention of Robin's name, Gerald's face lit up.

"Maybe you are underestimating him. . . . He's the first sorcerer I've met who's as skilled with the Graphems as he is with a computer keyboard!"

"Robin is an apprentice," Quadehar corrected him, "not a sorcerer yet. . . ."

"When someone is able to open a door locked tight with a powerful spell by creating a computer in the dirt and hacking into a system protected by a program written by me, he deserves to be promoted to Chief Sorcerer immediately," retorted Gerald.

"Yes, if you say so. . . ." Quadehar smiled in spite of himself.

Since the incident in the subterranean corridors of Gifdu when Robin had stood up to Lord Sha by weaving a spell beyond the capabilities of even chief sorcerers, Quadehar had also been wondering whether there was any limit to his apprentice's abilities.

"But that doesn't solve my problem. . . ." he added.

Gerald pondered, then suddenly snapped his fingers.

"I've got an idea!"

He turned to Bertram.

"Bertram and Robin have been getting on like a house on fire. I'm right, aren't I, Bertram?"

"Yes, Master. You're absolutely right," agreed the young sorcerer with a big grin.

"Why not make Bertram Robin's bodyguard, then? He's proved that he's both brave and able, by raising the alarm under Lord Sha's very nose. Officially, he could be sent by the Guild to work with your apprentice in your absence. What do you say, Bertram?"

"You want to make me that brat's official minder?" exclaimed Bertram, secretly both flattered by this responsibility and thrilled at the idea of seeing Robin again. "Well! That's fine with me. I accept!"

"It's a good idea," admitted Quadehar.

"Perfect!" concluded Gerald, rubbing his hands together. "Quadehar, go and pack your bags. We're going to plan your escape. Meanwhile, I'm going to produce a fake certificate from the Guild appointing Bertram to supervise Robin!"

Quadehar, reassured by the turn of events, returned to his room with a light step. As he wrote out the certificate, Gerald lectured Bertram on his responsibilities. And Bertram could only think of one thing, which was that life outside Gifdu with Robin would be far more exciting than even *he* could imagine!

21

TWO OLD FRIENDS

"You asked to see me, Urian?"

"Yes, Valentino. Come and sit down."

Lord Penmarch's butler sat down on the fireside stool where he liked to keep the old warrior company in the evenings as he stared into the leaping flames, reminiscing. Urian was certainly in a talkative mood. Valentino knew him inside out — they had been boys together at Bromotul, together on the roads of The Lost Isle and on the paths of The Uncertain World. Together now for so many years . . .

The old soldier would begin talking when he was ready, Valentino told himself, and settled down patiently to wait.

"I'm bored," said Urian at length. "I'm bored and I'm stuck in a rut. There's no action in my life, nothing going on."

"Come, come. Admittedly, your life now is different from what it used to be, but you've never complained before. What's the matter with you?"

Urian heaved a great sigh.

"It's since I visited Romaric at Bromotul. It was like seeing myself when I was his age. Worst of all, I feel as though the years since then have just flown past!"

The dancing flames cast their orange and yellow reflections on the bushy gray beard of the giant warrior, sunk in his huge armchair.

Opposite him, Valentino smiled to see his friend plagued by nostalgia. The butler, with his bony features, white hair, and tall, wiry frame, was a striking contrast to Urian, who was all stout flesh and muscle. But the differences did not stop there. . . .

They had both been adolescents in the days when you had to be from one of the noble families to join the Brotherhood, so they had entered Bromotul by different routes. Urian, the eldest Penmarch, had been accepted as a squire, while Valentino, the youngest child from an ordinary Dashtikazar family, was taken on as a kitchen boy.

One day, infuriated by the contemptuous attitude of some of the squires toward him, Valentino had challenged several of them to a duel and had got the better of them. The Chief Knight of Bromotul was so impressed with Valentino's bravery that he offered to take him out of the kitchens and train him as a squire, on the condition that one of the noble squires agreed to champion him. Only Urian had come forward, deaf to the objections of his peers, for he was convinced that the only true nobility was that of the heart. Valentino had been deeply grateful, and the two had become firm friends.

Later, when the two men had decided to team up as knights, they were nicknamed Don Quixote and Sancho Panza, because of their appearance, their idealism, and their friendship.

When the time came for them to take a backseat and make

room for younger, more vigorous knights, Urian naturally invited Valentino to come and live at Penmarch with him. That all seemed long ago. . . .

Valentino's eyes lit up. "Don Quixote and Sancho Panza . . . do you remember?"

A smile crept over Urian's glum face.

"Of course I do! The number of fights we got into because of those nicknames. And then eventually, we came to see them as a compliment!"

"You were head and shoulders above everyone when it came to wielding a hatchet. And the lance! How many opponents did you defeat in tournaments?"

"What about you, you were an outstanding fencer. How many upstarts did you put in their place with your foil?"

The two men became more and more animated as they relived the old days.

"It was only in The Uncertain World that we found adversaries who were a match for us," concluded Valentino, nodding.

"I'm still smarting from the memory of the blow I received on the arm from that giant Ork," mused Urian.

"That was outside Ferghana, when we were pursuing the Wanderer who was threatening to destroy The Door on the Middle Island, wasn't it?"

"Yes . . . What adventures we had, by Jove, what adventures!"

Urian thumped the arm of his chair. "But what about now, Valentino?" he moaned. "I spend my time eating, daydreaming, and sleeping, like just about everyone else on The Lost Isle! Brooding in my armchair while The Shadow is plotting and scheming against us . . ."

"Come, come, Urian," Valentino attempted to soothe him. "We did what we had to do, now it's up to others to act. . . ."

"Nonsense!" thundered Urian. "It's all in the hands of the Guild these days! The Guild makes all the decisions, calls the shots. The Brotherhood is nothing but a poodle, meekly obeying the Sorcerers! No, by Jove! The Shadow may be a devilish creature, but all the same it was physical force, not magic tricks, that defeated him every time! Do you remember, in the Golden Mountains . . . ?"

Visions of heaps of bodies on a road, jubilant Orks, and a sinister shape trailing a dark shadow in its wake flooded into Valentino's mind. With a shudder, he shook his head to dispel the image.

"Do you realize, my dear Valentino," went on Urian in a desperate voice, "that The Lost Isle is reduced to sending mere kids to fight The Shadow! Kids!"

"That's not quite what happened," objected Valentino. "Romaric and his friends went off on their own initiative to find the Balangru girl, unbeknownst to the authorities. . . ."

"You're quibbling! What I mean is that there are no men worthy of the name left on The Lost Isle, and now we expect kids to do our job for us!"

"They're not as helpless as all that," protested Valentino. "Apparently Robin destroyed Thunku's palace with a single magic word. . . ."

"Nonsense!" roared Urian. "Quadehar was there! It was he who did it and Robin took all the credit!"

"You are being unfair," sighed the butler. "Your dislike of

that boy blinds you. After all, he's your nephew, and it's not his fault —"

"He's the son of that coward, that traitor!"

"And of your sister."

"Sadly for me and for the name of Penmarch!"

Urian had gone purple in the face. Valentino knew that at this point in the conversation it was useless to try and reason with his friend.

And yet, he would so have liked to have persuaded Urian to be kinder to Robin, who was being made to suffer for his father's misdemeanors. He felt a kinship with this boy, who was rejected as he had been, and forced to accomplish great feats to gain recognition, while for others it was just a matter of birth. . . .

He rose and walked away from the hearth, leaving the giant to wallow in his melancholy thoughts.

22
A DARK, STORMY NIGHT

Quadehar chose to leave the Monastery of Gifdu on a night when a storm was rumbling. First of all, because darkness was always the best cover for this sort of exploit, and secondly, because the thunderclaps that rang through the old building drowned out the unavoidable sounds that accompany any escape. Like that of a sharp blow to the back of a head, a groan, and a body slumping onto the flagstone floor in the corridor . . .

Quadehar checked that the sorcerer stationed outside the door of his room hadn't attracted attention when he fell. Then he grabbed him by the feet, dragged him inside, and laid him on the bed, making sure that he was only temporarily stunned, then covered him with the blanket.

Then he crept silently down the corridor and made for the courtyard and the main entrance, locked from the inside by a collective spell.

"Gerald?" the sorcerer called soundlessly.

"I'm here," replied the computer wizard inside his head. "Are you ready?"

"I'm ready."

Quadehar stepped back. Controlled from Gerald's computer, the door creaked, then began to open with a ghastly grating sound, partly drowned by a timely rumbling in the sky.

"Can you squeeze through?"

"I'll manage. Lucky I'm not fat, unlike some!"

"Don't mock! Sitting at a computer all day doesn't do much for one's waistline! I'm not fortunate enough to exercise all the time like you, racing up and down towers and fleeing from monasteries!"

Quadehar couldn't help smiling.

"Stop complaining or I'll force you to come on this mission!"

"In that case, I won't keep you. Good luck, old chap."

"Thank you, my friend."

Their telepathic conversation stopped. Quadehar invoked Dagaz, the Graphem of psychic invisibility, and made it float above him with a Mudra. He slipped outside and set off along the path to the gorge with a joyful step. When the rain began to bucket down, he pulled the hood of his sorcerer's cloak up over his head.

≋ ✳ ≋ ✳ ≋

"What the devil's going on?" bawled Urian Penmarch, opening his bedroom door. He had been awakened from his slumbers by a loud banging on the door of his castle.

"I think somebody needs to shelter from the storm," replied Valentino, clad in an old dressing gown and swinging a lantern.

"Open up, for heaven's sake! I'll go and poke the fire. In this storm, whoever it is must be soaked through!"

There was a very strong tradition of hospitality on The Lost Isle. Anyone overtaken by nightfall or caught in bad weather could ask for shelter anywhere, at any house. Board and lodging were always guaranteed, even by the humblest of families, who considered it a duty to help anyone in trouble.

Generally, however, a stranger passing through would turn to the nearest Qamdar, or clan chief, who was generally in a better position to provide shelter than other people. "Wealth should be put to better use than giving parties and drinking in the best taverns!" was one of Urian's favorite sayings. For actually, beneath his fierce exterior, he was always willing to help those in need.

Valentino drew back the bolts, and a dripping wet Quadehar hurried into the entrance hall.

"Whew! Out of the rain at last!" exclaimed the sorcerer, shaking himself.

"Give me your cloak and go into the dining room," the butler gently directed him, deciding to save his questions for later. "Urian's already in there rekindling the fire."

"Thank you, Valentino."

Quadehar entered the vast room, where Urian was poking around in the hearth.

"Quadehar!" exclaimed the giant, noticing him at last. "What a surprise! Come over here and dry yourself in front of the fire!"

He tossed a bundle of dry beechwood onto the glowing embers and it crackled, sending flames shooting up. The sorcerer sat down on a stool and stretched his legs out in front of the fire.

"I've been dreaming of this moment! Finally some peace and freedom," Quadehar smiled.

Lord Penmarch seated himself in his armchair while Valentino joined them with a steaming pot of tea.

"Thank you, Valentino," he added, taking the cup the butler held out to him.

"By Jove! What are you doing outdoors on a night like this?" asked Urian in amazement.

"If I tell you, you might throw me out again."

"You intrigue me, Quadehar!"

"My dear Urian, you have opened your door to a prisoner on the run. An outlaw. An outcast from the Guild."

Valentino turned pale.

"What do you mean?"

"I may as well tell you the whole story. A few days ago, the Guild launched an operation against The Shadow deep inside The Uncertain World, which I had the privilege to lead. But the attack ended in a massacre and I was the only one to come back alive. The Guild holds me responsible for the disaster, and locked me up at Gifdu. I escaped earlier this evening."

Urian and Valentino sat there dumbfounded for a moment. Then the elderly warrior thumped the arm of his chair vigorously with his fist.

"By Jove! Quadehar, you've certainly come to the right place. My castle is your castle! The Guild won't find you here, I swear it!"

"But I don't understand, Quadehar," broke in Valentino. "It doesn't make sense. You're the Guild's finest sorcerer and everybody knows it. Could this be a plot against you? To prevent your succeeding Charfalaq?"

"That had occurred to me, but I'm not sure, even if my worst enemy, the Chief Sorcerer of Gri, does covet the position of the Chief Sorcerer . . . the Guild thinks that the operation failed because of a traitor. The fact that I'm the only one to have survived counts against me. The Guild didn't look any further. I'm the perfect culprit."

"That's preposterous!" exclaimed Urian.

"What *is* so preposterous," agreed Quadehar, after taking a sip of tea, "is to suspect me. What isn't so outrageous, however, is to think that there might be a traitor within the Guild. And I'd go even further . . ."

Urian and Valentino exchanged an anxious look.

"What do you mean?"

"I mean," announced Quadehar calmly, "that the Guild itself is perhaps victim of a plot, and that The Shadow has probably been receiving information from someone inside for a long time."

"I knew it!" thundered Urian. "I told you so, Valentino! That darned Guild is too powerful! And if The Shadow is somehow controlling it as well . . ."

"Calm down, Urian," broke in Quadehar. "I didn't say that The Shadow was controlling the Guild, but that he probably has spies within it!"

"Why do you think there's a plot?" queried Valentino, astounded.

"And there's something else," went on Quadehar, ignoring the question. "You won't believe me . . . but Yorwan is alive! He now calls himself Sha. Lord Sha! He turned up at Gifdu while I was in The Uncertain World. And he chased Robin through the vaults of the monastery . . ."

Quadehar thought Urian was going to choke. Valentino thumped him hard on the back.

"What?" he roared. "What did you say? He's still alive?"

"Shut up, Urian," snapped Valentino. "Quadehar hasn't finished."

Still spluttering, Urian sat down again, his face purple with rage. The sorcerer continued. "Apparently, Yorwan and I both went off on a wild goose chase at the same time. Somebody seems to be amusing himself sending us in the wrong direction. Anyway . . . I don't know exactly what happened when Yorwan caught Robin, but it appears he wasn't the boy that he was seeking," concluded Quadehar, bowing his head.

The two retired knights sat thunderstruck. Valentino was the first to recover his wits. "You mean . . . you mean that Robin isn't Yorwan's son?"

"Absurd!" burst out Urian. "Yorwan was my sister's fiancé! Robin must be his child!"

The huge old warrior rose and began pacing up and down to calm his terrible anger.

"That's what I always believed, too," Quadehar said to Valentino, lowering his voice, "and I thought that explained Robin's special talent for magic. With a father like Yorwan . . ."

"I never did understand what happened," said Valentino softly, making sure that Urian was out of earshot. "Yorwan seemed so desperately in love with Alicia. He broke his vows of celibacy and even left the Guild for her. So why was he so stupid as to steal the *Book of the Stars*, on the eve of their wedding?"

"Nobody has ever understood," said the sorcerer. "But now, I think we have to seek the real reason behind Yorwan's behavior!"

"A reason that has something to do with the plot you mentioned earlier?"

"Perhaps . . ."

"Alicia must know something," announced Urian darkly, planting himself squarely before them. "I'm going to see her right away. By Jove! She'd better speak out!"

"Sit down, Urian," ordered Quadehar authoritatively. "I'm sure Alicia won't be able to tell us anything of real importance. No, the answer to our questions lies elsewhere."

"Where then?" asked Urian, defeated, sinking back into his armchair.

"In The Uncertain World, my friends! What would you say to a little trip to the land of Orks and brigands?"

Incredulous at first, Urian's face suddenly lit up.

"Now you're talking, Quadehar! Valentino — get our weapons from the cupboard! By Jove and by Jupiter, some action at last!"

Valentino looked intently at Quadehar. Then, seeing that he wasn't joking, permitted himself a huge smile.

Life was becoming exciting again at least!

23
THE PRECIOUS BOOK OF SPELLS

"At last . . . at last it's in my hands . . . my Book, the Book I've wanted for so many years . . ."

Standing before a massive table in the center of the room where he liked to sit, the shadowy figure caressed the yellowing pages of a book of spells bound in black leather and studded with stars.

"Spells, such powerful spells . . . they are all here . . . waiting for me . . . for my glory . . . but it is too soon. It is still too soon. . . ."

The figure closed the book of spells and ran his fingers down the spine. Fragments of shadow remained here and there, where his hands had been.

"I still need the boy . . . but he'll be here soon enough . . . to help raise me to my rightful status . . . assist me in my conquest . . ."

The hollow whisperings dissolved into a chilling laugh.

"Master?"

"Yes, Lomgo . . . What do you want . . . ?"

Still the figure had not turned around. The scribe bowed and replied, "The men who went to the Uncertain South are back at last, Master."

"Send them in . . . Lomgo, my loyal Lomgo . . . Lomgo . . . ?"

"Master?"

"You have served your master well in stealing the Book back from our old friend. . . . You will not be forgotten, I promise you . . ."

"Thank you, Master," replied the scribe, who resembled a bird of prey. He stood aside to make way for a disheveled and tired-looking group of three men with shaven heads, dragging behind them a boy who was bound hand and foot.

"Master," began one of them, "beyond the deserts, we found a boy who matched the description exactly."

The figure turned around and scrutinized the boy with green eyes, who lay prostrate on the floor, trembling. The three men looked away.

"Idiots . . . get that brat out of here. . . . Haven't you heard? . . . I've found the child, the right one. . . . All by myself . . . I found him in another World. . . ."

The men looked at each other in dismay.

"Get out of here, I tell you . . . before I get rid of you myself. . . ."

They didn't wait to hear more and hurried off down the stairs, dragging the boy with them.

The shadowy figure once again concentrated his attention on the Book.

"At last . . . at last, I have it. . . ."

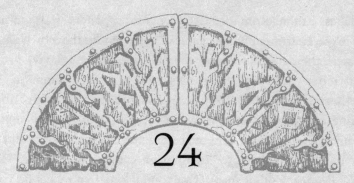

24

SAMAIN

The Samain holidays, at the beginning of November, lasted for three days. Traditionally, the first of these days was devoted to the ancestors and their memory, which was kept alive by visiting the cemeteries and politely listening to parents' and grandparents' tales of bygone times.

The other two days were much more fun: All the school-children and students of The Lost Isle came to Dashtikazar, the capital, to celebrate the end of summer and lament the long wait until its return, with games and dancing. At this time, and especially during the carnival, when they symbolically "burned" winter, the Provost ordered the knights, whose job was to maintain law and order in the streets, to be especially lenient.

To escape the noisy festivities, the older inhabitants would go and stay with relatives or friends in the country and, following a very old custom, they'd build bonfires in the hills and sit around them swapping memories.

Having paid tribute to their ancestors in their respective

villages, Robin, Romaric, Godfrey, Amber, and Coral had met up in the apartment in the center of town lent to them by Utigern Krakal, the twins' father, for the duration of the holiday.

"Godfrey, can you stop for a minute?" moaned Romaric.

"Sorry," replied Godfrey, strumming the strings of his zither, sitting cross-legged on the rug in the center of the vast dining room. "The Academy told me to practice my scales every day."

"Go onto the balcony, then," sighed the young squire. "We can't hear each other speak with you making that racket on your guitar!"

"I can't," went on Godfrey, unmoved. "There's too much noise outside. And for your information, it's not a guitar, it's a zither."

On the streets below, groups of young people were laughing and calling to each other as they went up the street toward Dashtikazar's main square.

"Leave him alone," warned Robin. "It's important for him . . ."

"Yes," added Coral, "and the sooner he's finished practicing the quicker he'll shut up!"

"You're a bunch of ignoramuses!" retorted Godfrey from the corner of the room where he had retreated.

"Yeah, yeah, Mozart, that's right," replied Romaric. "Just be grateful that we don't tie you to a chair to get some peace and quiet!"

Amber came back from the kitchen with a plate of sandwiches.

Godfrey immediately abandoned his zither and joined the starving group.

"Well, well," grinned Romaric. "I thought your mind was on higher things."

"Didn't you say you had to practice your scales?" teased Amber.

"Are you all ganging up on me, or what?" burst out Godfrey half-irritably. "I'm the only one who's got to work, so I'm the only one who should be allowed to eat!"

Coral came up behind him and ruffled his hair.

"Stop it! I hate that!"

Grumpily, Godfrey smoothed his hair, glowering at the others, which of course was a signal for them to do it all over again. His friends allowed him to get up only when his hair was a complete mess.

"OK, you win, I'm stopping for today," Godfrey gave in with a laugh. "But it'll be your fault if the Academy kicks me out!"

"We'll risk it," said Romaric.

"Anyway," concluded Coral, "you wouldn't have been able to play for long. It's getting dark and it's nearly time for the Jeshtan hunt!"

Just then, there was a knock at the front door. The five friends looked at each other.

"Are you expecting somebody?" asked Amber.

The others shook their heads, but Robin, unnoticed by the others, suddenly turned pale.

Oh no, he thought. *I hope that's not Agatha!*

Amber went to open the door.

A strange, sturdy character wearing a sorcerer's cloak stood framed in the doorway. He held his head high and surveyed them with a superior air. He had a goatee and a thin moustache.

"Bertram!" exclaimed Robin, rushing to greet him. "What on earth are you doing here?"

"I'll explain," promised Bertram, warmly shaking Robin's hand. "Aren't you going to introduce me to your friends?"

"Er . . . yes, yes, of course. Bertram, this is my cousin Romaric; he's a squire at Bromotul."

"All brawn and no brain, I suppose," sneered the sorcerer, raising an eyebrow in distaste and holding out a reluctant hand to Romaric, who stood there speechless.

"And, er, this is Godfrey," continued Robin, feeling uncomfortable. "He's from Bounic and he's studying at the Tantreval Academy of Music."

"A bumpkin who plays the bagpipes!" jeered Bertram, looking him up and down.

"This is Coral, Utigern Krakal's daughter," Robin went on quickly before Godfrey could reply.

Bertram rested his gaze on Coral and stood there open-mouthed.

"What a beauty! Allow me to kiss your pretty hand, Miss!"

"You will do nothing of the kind. You leave my sister alone," ordered Amber, her fists on her hips and her eyes blazing.

"Er . . . and this is Amber, Coral's —" stammered Robin.

"Now, she's kind of cute!" exclaimed Bertram, glancing at Amber with her cropped hair. "And what a haircut — she's got character, too!"

Bertram didn't have the chance to say another word. Amber kneed him in the stomach. He doubled up in pain and fell moaning onto the carpet.

"Well done, Amber!" cried Godfrey ecstatically.

"I worship you!" added Romaric adoringly.

"Are you crazy? What's got into you?" protested Coral. "He only wanted to kiss my hand to pay tribute to my beauty!"

"He can start by paying tribute to the carpet," retorted Amber frostily before turning to Robin. "Do you know this character?"

"There must be some mistake," said Robin defensively. "He's Bertram, a sorcerer from Gifdu. He's not usually like this. . . . Well, not exactly! I don't understand."

"Hey, I think he's trying to say something!" called out Coral, who had gone over to Bertram, still doubled up and groaning rather theatrically on the floor.

The young sorcerer was clutching his stomach with one hand and was waving the other desperately in Robin's direction. He was apparently having difficulty forming his words.

"You're right, Coral," agreed Romaric. "I think he's trying to tell us something."

"It's sad watching a worm trying to communicate," chipped in Godfrey.

"I think we should put him out of his misery and squash him with our heels," suggested Romaric.

"Excellent idea," approved Godfrey.

"Shut up, the two of you," snapped Robin, bringing his ear close to Bertram's lips.

"Here we go," sighed Godfrey. "Our Robin just can't help going to the rescue! I think we need a leader with more *oomph*. Amber, for example!"

"I couldn't agree more," went on Romaric.

"Shut up!" barked Robin. "I can't hear what he's saying!"

"Joking . . . I . . . sense of humor . . . Where I come from people . . . can take a joke. . . ."

"Is he begging for a quick and painless death?" asked Godfrey hopefully.

"Or a lawyer to make his last will and testament?" said Romaric.

Bertram had grabbed Robin by the collar as he continued to translate for his friends.

"Something serious . . . Quadehar . . . replac . . ."

Then, suddenly, Bertram recovered his breath and his voice:

"QUADEHAR SENT ME HERE! SOMETHING TERRIBLE HAS HAPPENED TO HIM! HE'S ASKED ME TO REPLACE HIM AS YOUR MENTOR!"

"And before?" asked Romaric quietly, while Robin backed away weakly. "What were you saying?"

"IT WAS A JOKE. WHERE I COME FROM, PEOPLE CAN TAKE A JOKE. THEY HAVE A SENSE OF HUMOR!"

25

THE JESHTAN HUNT

"Hurry up," urged Coral, wringing her hands. "We're going to miss the Jeshtan hunt!"

"Wait a minute," soothed Godfrey. "Robin isn't ready yet."

"Robin," screeched Coral impatiently, heading down the stairs. "Hurry up!"

Robin was sitting on the living room floor, still in a state of shock from Bertram's news. The sounds of the joyful clamor from the street reached their ears through the big open bay window. Amber and Romaric were sitting by his side trying to persuade him to join them, watched by a bemused Bertram, who now kept a safe distance from Amber.

"Come on, Robin! I know what's happened to Master Quadehar is serious . . . but staying here and brooding won't change anything," coaxed Romaric.

"He's right, Robin," said Amber. "Come on! It's the first time the five of us have all been together since the summer holidays.

Don't spoil things, like that idiot's been trying to do since he got here. . . ."

"The idiot in question is named Bertram," ventured the sorcerer, raising his hand.

"Your name's as ridiculous as your moustache and that face fungus on your chin," retorted Amber cuttingly.

"Listen," Bertram said with a sigh. "Let's start again. I'm sorry about what happened. It's my way of joking and . . ."

"Bertram's right," broke in Robin. "What's happened to my master is bad enough as it is, without our petty squabbles. . . ."

"Ah, you see?" exulted Bertram.

"Petty squabbles . . . petty insults is more like it!" objected Romaric, glaring at the sorcerer.

"In any case," went on Bertram, recovering his customary arrogance, "I have here a document from the Guild placing Robin in my care. Whether you like it or not, I . . ."

"You know what you can do with your document?" scoffed Romaric.

"I should warn you," said Godfrey in his placid way. "Coral's going crazy on the stairs."

Robin made up his mind.

"All right," he grumbled, getting up. "I don't feel like partying but I'll come with you all the same. So will Bertram. I'm an apprentice sorcerer and I must obey my master's wishes. If he wants Bertram to protect me . . ."

"Precisely!" said Bertram, nodding his head emphatically.

"I suppose we can try and put up with him," conceded Amber, looking at Robin thoughtfully.

"OK," went on Godfrey. "But just a trial, then! Let's say just until this evening . . ."

At that moment, Coral burst into the apartment, preventing Bertram from saying anything else. "Come on! Unless you're really determined to ruin the Samain holidays!"

"We're coming, we're coming," laughed Romaric. "Robin was getting ready, and we couldn't decide what color eye shadow he should wear. . . ."

"Moron!" replied Robin, unable to suppress a smile.

"You took the words out of my mouth," said Bertram.

They all clattered down the staircase.

≋ ✳ ≋ ✳ ≋

In the street, groups of young people were charging around everywhere, shouting and laughing. The Jeshtan hunt, which kicked off the celebrations, had begun! According to legend, the Jeshtan was an evil gnome who raided the food stocks that the inhabitants of The Lost Isle had built up during the summer to see them through the winter. It was vital to track him down and put him out of action before winter set in. Now, every year, there was a special re-enactment.

"I saw him!" shrieked a girl. "Over there!"

The crowd rushed in the direction she was pointing.

"Quick, let's follow!" said Coral excitedly.

"We're off!" replied Godfrey, running alongside her.

The four others followed behind less enthusiastically.

"Imprisoning Master Quadehar!" snorted Robin furiously. "They have no right!"

139

"And you say, Bertram, that the Guild tried Quadehar like a common criminal?" asked Romaric.

"Yes," replied Bertram, who had obviously decided to be as friendly as possible. "The only person who tried to defend him was Gerald, my former master. At the end, the Chief Sorcerer, Charfalaq, looked very upset, but the Council went ahead and suspended Master Quadehar from office. . . ."

"It doesn't make sense!" declared Amber. "If it was Sha who was behind the Jaghatel massacre, why didn't he kill the Gifdu sorcerers? And why didn't he kidnap Robin?"

Robin did not answer immediately. Of course, he hadn't told his friends everything, neither what Agatha had told him last summer about Sha, who was searching for his lost son, nor about the Lord of Jaghatel's mysterious words, and even less the story of Yorwan, the thief who had stolen the *Book of the Stars*.

Bertram spoke for him, puffing himself up. "It's thanks to me that Robin was able to escape! With extraordinary courage I —"

"I find this whole business strange, too," Robin cut in as Romaric and Amber exchanged a look of exasperation. "But one thing is clear, and that is that the Guild has got it wrong."

"In convicting Quadehar?" asked Romaric.

"Obviously . . ."

A sudden commotion around them cut their conversation short — the Jeshtan had been flushed out. Amber, Robin, Bertram, and Romaric joined in, allowing themselves to be swept along by the crowd. They ran through the streets mingling with the other teenagers of The Lost Isle.

Soon, in the main square of Dashtikazar, which was lit by

hundreds of torches, a group of whooping girls brandished aloft the figure of a grimacing gnome.

"Huh!" sniffed Coral scornfully. "They were lucky, that's all."

Their little group had met up on one side of the square by a marble fountain shaped like a giant shell.

They joined the procession as it wound its way up to the palace of the Provost, who was both mayor of Dashtikazar and prefect of The Lost Isle. There, under the benign gaze of the amused knights on sentry duty, the girls who had found the straw-and-rag Jeshtan slipped a noose around the scarecrow's neck and hung him from a lamppost to a storm of applause and cheers.

Then, the knights threw scary masks and gruesome figurines down to the throngs of young people outside the palace. Those who caught them set off through the streets wearing the masks or brandishing the stuffed dummies. At midnight, they would decorate the town's lampposts with them, where they would stay until the end of Samain, to warn the evil spirits of the fate that awaited them if they ventured onto The Lost Isle!

Godfrey had put on an ogre's mask made of cardboard and, to Coral and Romaric's delight and Bertram's disdain, was having fun frightening the younger children by prancing around diabolically amid the general chaos. A little farther away, behind them, Amber was keeping Robin company. The apprentice could not help feeling depressed.

"It'll be all right," she tried to reassure him. "Everybody knows that Quadehar is an extraordinary man. The Commission's investigation will exonerate him."

"That's not all," sighed Robin.

"What else is there, then?"

"It's . . ." replied Robin, who was reluctant to let Amber in on the secret. "It's that life seems to have got incredibly complicated since Uncle Urian's birthday party! I should never have fainted. . . ."

"Well, you couldn't do much about that. But it's true that many things changed afterward! And not only for you . . ."

"What do you mean?"

"I mean," hesitated Amber, glancing sideways at him, "what I mean is, I . . . no, forget it."

"Do you mean the dreams you mentioned in your letters?" asked Robin innocently, unaware of Amber's embarrassment.

"No. I mean, yes. Sort of."

"Well?"

"We'll talk about it tomorrow. Let's just enjoy ourselves this evening! It's nice being like this, the two of us . . . I mean, all five of us together, isn't it? Despite the presence of that stuck-up bodyguard of yours!"

"Bertram's really nice, believe me; he's just a bit shy and awkward. Give him a chance! But it's true, you're right, I'm spoiling the fun with my long face. Come on, let's join the others."

They caught up with Coral and Bertram, who made himself scarce as soon as he saw Amber coming, then the little group found Romaric and Godfrey hanging Godfrey's mask from a lamppost. Afterward, they headed off to the beach where a big bonfire was already burning.

They went over to a huge basket containing hundreds of white pebbles. They each took one and wrote their name on it with fireproof ink. Then they threw their stones into the flames. If the fire didn't shatter the pebble and they found it intact the next day, it would be a good omen for the coming year. Bertram joined in wholeheartedly and managed not to make any stupid comments.

They were hailed by some young people from the village of Krakal, who had recognized Amber and Coral, and the little gang joined the group for a moment. Then they walked in silence along the beach, with Bertram hanging back a little, happy simply to be together.

When the dampness of the night made them feel chilly, they decided to go back to the apartment in the center of town where they drank steaming mugs of apple cider, the light honey drink of The Lost Isle. Coral, Romaric, and Godfrey clinked glasses with Bertram, who launched into a funny and passionate speech about how he really wanted to be their friend.

"If you want to be Romaric's friend," said Godfrey quietly in his ear, "stop eyeing Coral the way you do and try not to hang around her. . . ."

Bertram, in a fierce whisper, denied having such designs, but reddened slightly. Then Amber and Robin joined them and they chatted about this and that, until they were tired enough to climb into their sleeping bags.

26

A BAD OMEN

"You snore really loudly, Bertram," exclaimed Amber, crawling out of her sleeping bag. "You're a pain at night and during the day!"

"That's nonsense. I don't snore," retorted the sorcerer in a sleepy voice, huddling under the blankets they'd lent him.

"Oh, yes you do, Bertram," said Robin, grinning as he set the table for breakfast. "Come on everybody, get up!"

"Up, you lazy creatures!" echoed Romaric, who was keeping an eye on the milk pan on the stove. "It's a gorgeous day outside!"

Robin opened the curtains and the sun flooded into the big room where they had all slept on mattresses on the floor. Godfrey, Bertram, and Coral groaned and buried their heads under their pillows. Amber, in her red pajamas, leaped up and kicked the others.

"There, you bogus sorcerer, that's for snoring last night! And that's for endlessly twanging the guitar, Godfrey! And you,

Sis, that's for all the times you've kept me waiting for the bathroom!"

"Oh, go away, Amber! You're not funny!" Coral moaned.

Amber joined Robin and Romaric at the table.

Gradually, the others got up and came and sat down too, grumbling and groaning at being woken up so violently.

"What are we doing today?" yawned Coral.

"This evening, dancing around the fire in the main square," replied Romaric, stirring his hot chocolate.

"Sh'afternoon," went on Robin, chewing a huge hunk of bread spread with peanut butter, "itsh 'e games of 'kill in 'e shtadium."

"What about this morning?" asked Bertram, scratching his bottom.

"This morning, we've got to go and get our pebbles from the beach," Amber reminded them, grimacing as she watched Robin smearing peanut butter everywhere.

"In that case . . . dibs I use the bathroom first!" said Coral, leaping up.

"No way!" yelled the other four, dropping what they were doing and rushing over to stop her.

Only the astonished Bertram remained at the table.

≋ ✳ ≋ ✳ ≋

When they were washed and dressed, they left the apartment and set off for the beach.

The narrow, winding streets were dark — the buildings on either side of the road were four or five stories high, and the sun wasn't yet high enough in the sky to properly light the pale granite paving stones.

It felt rather gloomy, so they were relieved to reach the beach around which the city of Dashtikazar lay curled. It was still early and most of the schoolchildren and students were still asleep, having partied late into the night.

The gang walked over to the fire, which was still smoldering in places. They poked among the embers with branches, and spread the hot ashes on the sand, then rummaged around for their pebbles. Coral was the first to find hers, lying next to Bertram's.

"My white stone's still intact!" she exclaimed happily.

"So is mine," replied Bertram, showing it to her and smiling. "It's a sign!"

"A sign of what?" interrupted Romaric, a little menacingly.

"Well . . ." stammered Bertram, who had seen Romaric barechested the night before when they were going to bed, and had concluded that he wouldn't stand a chance against him in a fight. "It's a good luck omen! For me! That I found my stone intact!"

"I've found mine," announced Godfrey. "It's all in one piece, too."

"Me, too," said Robin, blowing the ashes off the pebble he was holding.

"Mine's shattered," declared Amber, looking forlorn.

They gathered in silence around her as she clutched a fragment of stone on which half her name was visible.

"It's not important," Robin tried to console her.

"Oh, yes it is," replied Coral, distraught. "You have no idea!"

"She's right, it's a bad sign," said Amber gravely.

On seeing how upset her sister was, Coral walked determinedly over to the basket from which they had taken their white stones the day before, chose a pretty one, wrote "Amber" on it with the pen she wore on a string around her neck, and held it out to her. "Here, now we've all got our white stones intact."

Amber gave Coral a grateful look and kissed her affectionately on the cheek. Then she forced a smile and accepted the new pebble, throwing the old, shattered one into the embers.

"That's the way, Amber," said Bertram, who seized the chance to say something nice to her. "It's only a stone, after all."

She thanked him, and together they made their way back into town.

≋ ✳ ≋ ✳ ≋

"Now, tell me about these dreams of yours," Robin asked Amber when the two of them found themselves walking side by side, lagging behind the others as they made their way to the stadium where the games of skill marking the second day of the festival were to be held.

"Oh, you know, I told you everything in my letters," replied Amber after a silence. "Since I've been back from The Uncertain World, I've been having these weird dreams."

"Often?"

"Nearly every night."

"Are they always the same?"

"Yes, and no. I always dream about a vast forest. But then, the dreams change. Sometimes, I'm being chased by creatures that look like wild boar, but with dogs' heads. And sometimes,

I'm riding a horse, behind a woman with long hair and green eyes. Or I'm lying on a very hard bed and I hear a song that sends me to sleep. . . . The worst thing is that in these dreams, I feel as though I've really experienced all these things. But in real life, I've never been in that forest, and I've never met that woman."

Robin was puzzled.

"I don't know what to say, Amber. Perhaps the journey to The Uncertain World had a bad effect on you, as Master Quadehar already explained. . . . You remember your headache and sleeplessness when you arrived back?"

"I'm not likely to forget," grumbled Amber. "Only last month I was in bed with another of those headaches. By the way, thanks for writing to me."

"Oh, it was nothing. We have to be there for each other when times are hard. After all, we're friends, aren't we?"

"Yes, we're friends, good friends," said Amber, biting her lip.

There was a brief silence, then Amber blurted out, "All the same, I'm the only one who's been ill this year. And I was the only one to be affected by our stay in The Uncertain World! And then today, I'm the only one whose white pebble was shattered. . . ."

"Don't you think the one Coral gave you is just as good?" asked Robin, who didn't want her to get all upset again.

"Yes . . ." she replied, forcing herself to smile. "It'll do!"

"Why don't we talk to Bertram about your dreams?" suggested Robin. "He is a sorcerer, after all! He might have an idea."

"No," refused Amber, tossing her head prettily. "Not that I don't have faith in Bertram's skill, but . . . I'd rather keep it between ourselves. Like a secret."

She looked up at him with her deep blue eyes.

"As you like," stuttered Robin, suddenly feeling shy and awkward.

They caught up with their friends at an apple-bobbing stall.

"If you can pick one up with your teeth, it means you'll succeed in everything you do during the coming year!" announced Coral, flashing her dazzling white teeth.

She had her hands tied behind her back and tried to bob for an apple. She spluttered and choked, splashing madly. The young people standing around the tub made fun of her, while her friends egged her on. Eventually, Coral stood up, her head thrown back, dripping with water, and her teeth sunk into an apple that was almost choking her.

"Well done, Coral!" her sister congratulated her.

"Your turn, Bertram," ordered Romaric.

"Me? Why me?" asked the sorcerer in surprise.

"I want to be certain of something."

"Of what?" asked Bertram warily.

"You'll see. Go on, are you a wimp or what?"

Quick to rise to the challenge, Bertram put his hands behind his back and tried his luck, jeered at by some onlookers and cheered on by others. He, too, caught an apple, which he spat out disgustingly, then he struck a silly triumphant pose.

"Nobody else wants to try their luck?" asked Bertram wiping his face with a towel handed to him by one of the boys by the tub.

"No thanks," replied Godfrey. "I don't fancy getting a cold!"

"You mean you don't want to get your hair wet!" teased Coral, ruffling his hair.

"Oh, no!" exclaimed Godfrey, smoothing his hair. "Don't start that again!"

With that, Robin messed up his hair again and Godfrey fled, protesting loudly as his friends pursued him. Bertram grabbed Romaric's sleeve. "So, what did you want to be certain of, when you made me catch the apple?"

"That you wouldn't bring us bad luck," replied Romaric smugly, then marched off to join the others.

27

AMBER SEES RED

Later, when the sun's last rays faded and night descended over the second day of the holiday, the gang gathered around the big bonfire in the center of the main square.

While the musicians were warming up on the podium, Amber and Coral tried out a few steps with Romaric, who was still attempting to learn to dance, as Bertram looked on in amusement.

Then they ate heartily at the barbecue cooked by the knights over giant braziers.

As soon as the festivities began, Amber dragged Robin into the midst of the dancers and would not let him go. To avoid being invited to dance by a clumsy partner, as he usually was, Godfrey decided to take the initiative himself. He finally plucked up the courage and asked a girl to dance. First of all, he made her laugh with a few jokes, and then he managed to entice her away from her friends and onto the dance floor where they were dancing a medieval circle dance. Coral soon found herself alone with Bertram and Romaric.

"What a beautiful night!" she sighed, sitting on the edge of the shell-shaped pool and gazing up at the stars.

"Yes, it's a lovely night," agreed Bertram, thinking it was a great pity that Romaric was with them.

"It really is beautiful," added Romaric, silently cursing Master Quadehar for inflicting such an irritating sorcerer on them. He wasn't sure yet whether Bertram was simply ridiculous or down-right dangerous. "By the way, Bertram, is it true that sorcerers take vows of celibacy?"

"It is," replied Bertram grudgingly, raising an eyebrow. "But remaining unmarried doesn't mean you can't have a girlfriend," he added quickly, glancing furtively in Coral's direction.

Romaric grunted something about people playing games, but said no more. There was a heavy silence, which was suddenly broken by a figure bursting out from a side street.

"Hi, everyone! Is Robin with you? I've been looking all over for him since yesterday!"

"Agatha!" exclaimed Coral in surprise.

It was indeed Agatha. She was wearing a stunning outfit, and subtle makeup for a change. Romaric stared at her as if seeing her for the first time.

"Isn't Thomas with you?" he finally managed to say.

"Thomas, Thomas . . ." she replied, pulling a face. "Why are you always asking about Thomas? We're not joined at the hip you know!"

"No, but the two of you usually go everywhere together," protested Romaric.

He wondered why he'd never noticed that Agatha was rather pretty until now.

"I haven't introduced myself," broke in Bertram, stepping forward and bowing slightly. "Bertram, Sorcerer of the Guild and a friend of Robin's."

Agatha looked him up and down suspiciously. Then, realizing he was a real sorcerer and that this was not one of the gang's jokes, she nodded and held out her hand.

Bertram took it immediately and raised it dramatically to his lips.

"Oh, you're so gallant, Bertram!"

"How stupid!" retorted Coral, annoyed at not being the center of attention anymore.

Romaric felt quietly hopeful again.

"You know Bertram is a great sorcerer," he added for Agatha's benefit. "He's already saved Robin's life once!"

"Really?" was all Agatha had to say. "And where is Robin?" she added.

"He's dancing with Amber," replied Romaric irritably.

He had hoped that Agatha would be interested in Bertram who, in turn, would be distracted from Coral.

"Ah, yes, Amber . . ." murmured Agatha glumly.

"Ah, yes, Amber . . ." echoed Bertram, wincing at the memory of the kick in the stomach she'd given him the day before.

"Oh, so what!" said Agatha. "I'm not doing anything wrong, after all. I just want to have a chat with Robin. She doesn't own him!"

"A word of advice," ventured Romaric. "Be careful. I know Amber well, and subtleties like 'I just want to talk to him' don't go down too well with her."

"Even *I'd* say that my sister is quick to fly off the handle when it comes to Robin!" added Coral.

Coral was remembering Uncle Urian's birthday party, when Amber had slapped Agatha in front of everybody.

Agatha ignored this last remark. "Have a nice evening!" she trilled, as she turned on her heel.

She spotted Robin among the dancers as she threaded her way to the center of the square.

"We'd better follow her," suggested Romaric. "I think she's heading for trouble."

"Great!" grinned Coral. "I love it when my sister gets angry!"

"But tell me," inquired Bertram, dazed. "How come Robin's so good with the girls?"

"Oh! It's only recent," Romaric corrected him. "And to be honest, it's the girls who are running after *him*."

"Lucky guy!" Bertram sighed. "What's his secret?"

"Oh, couldn't be easier," smiled Romaric. "You simply thrash a few Gommons, knock out two or three Orks, and finish off by destroying the palace of the ruler of The Uncertain World. That's enough to wow them. Any other questions?"

Bertram held his tongue.

Meanwhile, Agatha was striding toward Robin, waving and shouting "Yoo-hoo!"

"Oh no, that looks like Agatha!" exclaimed Amber, who had stopped dancing and was watching the tall girl weave her way over to them.

"It's her, all right," said Robin, with a sinking feeling in his stomach.

The thing he'd been dreading most was about to happen. If only he knew a magic spell that could make the earth open and swallow him up, if there was such a thing. He promised himself he'd find one if he came out of this alive!

Amber greeted Agatha coolly.

"What are you doing here?"

"I've come to say hello to Robin," replied Agatha, taking no more notice of her, and flashing Robin a winning smile. "Hey Robin! How've you been since we last saw each other?"

"You last saw each other? When did you see her?" asked Amber quietly.

"Um, she means . . ." stammered Robin.

"You know, when we met in Penmarch!" said Agatha, ignoring Robin's frantic looks. "Robin, I just loved your room!"

Amber turned pale and stared at Robin with tear-filled eyes. Then she slowly turned her murderous gaze on Agatha.

"Come on, Amber, don't be silly," Robin ventured. "Agatha just dropped in to see me and we read comic books."

"You!" hissed Amber, with such a thunderous look that Agatha stared wide-eyed and stepped back a pace or two. "You wait until I get you!"

Amber hurled herself onto her rival, her claws out.

"Robin!" screamed Agatha, surrounded by the commotion of the dance, amazed at Amber's reaction. "Do something! She's going to kill me!"

Amber laughed strangely and Agatha broke away in a run.

"Amber, no!" yelled Robin, as Amber set off in pursuit.

He began to run after the girls.

"What's up?" shouted Romaric, as his cousin sped past him.

"It's Amber! She wants to strangle Agatha!"

Romaric set off after him, followed by Bertram and Coral. As they ran past Godfrey, they tore him away from his dance partner, who was left standing there open-mouthed, and quickly told him what had happened.

"That's love for you," commented Coral, excitedly racing along at Romaric's side.

"It's madness, that's what it is," snorted Romaric.

"What on earth got into her?" spluttered Godfrey, furious at having been forced to abandon his dance partner so rudely.

"Have you only just realized that Amber's completely insane?" panted Bertram.

The chase took them through the dark back streets. Soon, they had left the last houses of Dashtikazar behind them and were out on the open moors.

"This way!" yelled Robin.

They caught up with him and ran through the heather, guided by the moonlight. Suddenly, they heard Agatha scream.

"Too late," groaned Godfrey. "Either they're teasing us, or Amber's disemboweling Agatha!"

Then, suddenly, it was Amber who screamed.

"In any case . . ." gasped Bertram breathlessly, "it sounds as though Agatha's putting up a good fight."

They reached a big circle of charred grass and stopped in their tracks. Bertram and Robin exchanged looks.

"This is no joke. . . ." panted the junior sorcerer. "It's a dance circle. . . ."

"Korrigans!" confirmed Robin. "It's an ambush. Quick, let's get out of here!"

But before they could move, a net was thrown over them, and almost immediately a host of little hands, like cats' paws, were busy knotting the ends.

28

SNARED

"Robin! Do something!" shrieked Coral, as a Korrigan grabbed her.

Robin was in no state to answer, let alone do anything. Like Bertram, Romaric, Godfrey, Agatha, and Amber, he was bound hand and foot and his mouth was gagged with a wide strip of fabric. What use was it being a sorcerer if he had no way of calling on the magic signs that would release them? Robin was powerless, and so was Bertram, who rolled his eyes furiously. They could only helplessly witness their own kidnapping.

≋ ✳ ≋ ✳ ≋

The Korrigans had lived on the land long before people had settled there. Many years ago, before the storm that had caused The Lost Isle to break away from the coast of the mainland, the Korrigans used to plague the moors.

That was before the men of The Real World, forgetting the

Ancient Pact, hunted down and killed those who were not like them, before they destroyed the beauties of the world which they lived in, only to end up as sole survivors.

But here on The Lost Isle, humans had never had any difficulty cohabiting with this ancient species.

This was because the inhabitants of The Lost Isle lived in harmony with nature and considered themselves simply to be one type of creature among many. Unlike the people of The Real World, they had never thought of exterminating a race in order to take its place with their colonies and empires.

It was also because, luckily, humans and Korrigans rarely came into contact with each other. The Korrigans, who were content to stay on the moors, spent the nights dancing in a circle by the moonlight and their days feasting and enjoying themselves in their caves.

The Provost of Dashtikazar occasionally encountered Kor Mehtar, the Korrigan King, and the Chief Sorcerer of Gifdu sometimes received requests for arbitration from the Korrigans — who were great friends when it came to having fun, but were incapable of getting along with each other when it came to serious matters.

As for people who strayed onto the moors and found themselves in the wrong place at the wrong time, they were likely to pay the price of the little creatures' rather peculiar sense of humor. For example, the Korrigans would force their victims to dance all night, or make up the words to a song, or make the King laugh at a good joke. In exchange, they were rewarded for their performance, usually with a bag of gold coins if they'd been convincing, or egg on their faces if they weren't.

The schoolchildren of The Lost Isle were still taught the Korrigans' language from an early age, even though it was much more complicated than Ska, the tongue of The Uncertain World. It was considered part of their general education and also a courtesy toward their strange neighbors.

The Korrigans were short (between 2 and 3 feet tall), skinny, and wizened. But they were tremendously strong, and could carry a large dog on their shoulders for miles without tiring.

They had olive skin and were very hairy. Sometimes they plaited their hair, or concealed it under big hats. They had two tiny horns on their foreheads, a little wagging tail at the base of their spine, and hands like cats' paws. Copper buttons gleamed on their black jackets and they wore velvet pantaloons and iron shoes to complete their attire.

≈ ✳ ≈ ✳ ≈

The hostages' journey across the moor was only witnessed by the laughing moon. Robin, Romaric, Godfrey, Amber, Coral, Agatha, and Bertram were each carried by two Korrigans, one holding their feet and the other their arms. After what felt like an endless trek, their kidnappers stopped at the foot of a hill, at the top of which towered a dolmen.

The Korrigans' leader walked over to one of the stone pillars that supported the huge stone slab and placed his hand on a red-painted sign carved on the ridge. Robin, who was watching his every move, did not recognize the symbol. Then the leader muttered something in Korrigani, which the apprentice also couldn't catch. This was followed by a terrifying roar and the earth opened up at the foot of the pillar, revealing a stone staircase.

The motley group started its descent by the light of a gorse-branch torch carried by their guide.

They were soon in a narrow underground tunnel that smelled of mold and rotting timber.

Robin, bumped around by his bearers, tried one last time to loosen his bonds, but it was hopeless. He was furious with Amber. What on earth had got into her, attacking Agatha like that? The two girls should have sorted it out between them without some wild goose chase across the moor, but then he was partly to blame as well. If he had been more honest, they wouldn't have ended up in this situation, bound and gagged in the heart of the Korrigans' kingdom.

Robin wasn't exactly afraid, but feared that he and his friends would have to suffer the little creatures' love of practical jokes — or something worse!

If only they'd untie his hands!

Eventually, they reached a vast cavern, so big that it could have housed the whole of Penmarch castle! Thousands of glow-worms kept in jars standing in little niches in the rock face lit the walls that glistened with damp.

These little niches were cut into the rock walls and reached via a series of platforms, walkways, and log staircases. Dozens of Korrigans were sitting in them, their legs dangling over the sides, laughing and chatting. Everywhere else, they clustered in hundreds around crude tables, drinking, eating, and singing rowdy songs.

Some were playing: In one corner they were catapulting a ball into a net; in another, they were pushing a huge chunk of wood into the opposite camp, huffing and puffing for all they were worth; while in another corner, a daredevil was trying to balance on a wobbly beam, to the applause of a group of specta-tors. The air was filled with shouts of laughter.

"It's like Dashtikazar stadium in the middle of Samain," mused Robin, barely able to think over the din.

As they crossed the cavern, nobody seemed to pay them any attention or stop what they were doing. Once they reached the back of the cave, they were deposited on the ground and their gags and bonds were removed. Shaking themselves out and mas-saging their sore wrists, Robin and Bertram exchanged a glance. These Korrigans were in for a surprise! But before they could do anything, a voice chanted in Korrigani:

"Sorcerers of note you may well be
but if you're wise you'll listen to me.
Abandon all thought of magic in here
or live to regret your chosen career!"

The seven young people looked up. Perched on a throne hewn out of a huge rock, a Korrigan was looking them up and down with a mocking smile.

The gold crown on his head left no doubt as to his identity: They were in the presence of Kor Mehtar, the Korrigan King, a stern ruler and powerful magician himself.

The King burst out in a childish giggle and continued, still in Korrigani, the complicated rhyming language of the moorland people:

"Well, now, this is an unexpected treat," he cried, opening his arms and pointing at his toes,

"to have you groveling at my feet!
Here in Boulegant, my palace grand,
from which I govern this nether land!"

Kor Mehtar signaled to a cluster of Korrigans who vacated the table they were eating at, mumbling crossly. Then the King invited the friends to sit down.

"Yuck!" spluttered Agatha in disgust, pushing away a half-gnawed bone.

"Don't give it to us," complained Amber, glaring daggers at her.

But neither of them had the heart to continue their feud. After all, it was their fault they were all prisoners of the Korrigans.

Amber was quiet, almost calm. She couldn't say why she had lost her temper quite so violently with her rival. During the entire chase, she had felt as if she were somebody else. It wasn't the first time she had experienced that feeling. Each time she felt Robin was in danger, she reacted like that. Was that what love was all about? Hmmm. She had a slight headache coming on.

The King issued orders to a bunch of surly Korrigans who cleaned and then laid the table.

"A lot of good this will be if things turn ugly," moaned Romaric, holding a big wooden spoon that he'd been given along with a goblet and a plate.

"What are we going to do?" asked Amber, massaging her temples.

"Let's wait and see," he replied. "For the time being, they seem to be in a good mood. With a bit of luck, they'll let us go if we do their meal justice. . . ."

"I think it would be better to use our powers to get out of here," suggested Bertram, lowering his voice.

"Didn't you see Kor Mehtar?" objected Robin. "Somehow he knew immediately we were from the Guild, and it didn't seem to worry him one bit. He's said to be a great magician. . . . No, I think we should bide our time. . . . Let's behave like polite guests and see what happens."

There were brought huge pitchers of apple cider, which they poured into their pewter goblets. Then they were served a thick, dark stew. The Korrigans climbed onto the table to serve them, and their little iron shoes clattered on the hard wooden planks.

"The apple cider is delicious," said Godfrey, smacking his tongue appreciatively. "It tastes of fig."

"What's in this?" asked Coral anxiously, leaning over her plate filled with a rather unappealing broth.

"Try tasting it," replied Romaric, dipping his own spoon in and raising it to his mouth. "Ugh!" he spluttered, making a horrible face and turning bright red. "Watch out, it tastes of mold and it's very peppery!"

Kor Mehtar on his throne seemed to be having a good laugh at their expense.

"These Korrigans are incorrigible," Robin said with a sigh. "They are kind and cruel at the same time. The apple cider is delicious yet the food's disgusting. That just about sums up their sense of humor. . . ."

"Well, I don't think it's funny at all!" choked Bertram, who had also tasted the vile gruel. "I've never eaten anything so foul! Not even at Gifdu! It's a shameful insult, an affront!"

Their plight amused the King to no end. He exclaimed gleefully,

My dear guests why this dismal air?
Aren't you satisfied with our delicious fare?

Red with rage, Bertram rose and glared at Kor Mehtar.

"Don't do anything stupid!" begged Robin. "Please sit down!"

But Bertram was determined. He launched foolishly into the Korrigans' complicated language and got all tongue-tied.

"Kor Mehtar, you really are very sick
to play on your poor guests such a tasteless trick."

The King's smile had vanished. He growled back angrily,

"Mind your manners, you impudent fool
or I'll serve up something far worse than gruel!"

At that, Robin leaped to his feet to prevent things going from bad to worse.

"Please forgive him, Sire, he means no ill
languages have never been his skill."

Then, still angry, the King demanded:

"You who speak our tongue with ease,
introduce your six friends, if you please."

Robin concentrated and began,

"Bertram here thinks it's cool,
to lark around and play the fool."

"But I . . ." objected Bertram before Amber kicked his shin.

"Amber and Coral, twin sisters are,
one's a beauty, the other's a star," went on Robin, sweating profusely in his effort to speak Korrigani.

"My cousin Romaric's true and valiant,
Godfrey's the one with musical talent.
And Agatha, my friend over there . . ."

". . . looks like the back end of a bear," Amber couldn't help whispering.

"Doesn't have a curl in her hair," concluded Robin lamely, mopping his brow.

"As for me, O King so brave,
I am Robin, your humble slave."

The King, who had listened politely to Robin, sat up on his throne.

"Not Robin Penmarch the young wizard of great flair,
whose fame precedes him everywhere?" he insisted with a smile that lit up his dark, whiskered face.

"Aha! This is a splendid surprise,
now I shall be the one to claim the prize!"

He motioned to a group of Korrigans, who stopped their game and made their way toward the friends.

The seven prisoners exchanged anxious glances — what prize was he talking about?

29

THE CHALLENGE

Robin took a deep breath, determined to find out more.
"*Oh noble ruler of this land*," he ventured,
"*Tell me so I understand*
why you rubbed your hands with glee,
when you learned of my identity?"
The King gazed at him thoughtfully and replied:
"*Luck is on my side today,*
for I know someone who will pay
a king's ransom for your capture —
hence the reason for my rapture."
Robin noticed Bertram's hand inching gingerly toward his
sorcerer's bag, but then he evidently changed his mind.

"Let's put our heads together, there must be a way to escape,"
he whispered to Robin.

"No," replied the apprentice calmly. "There are really too many
of them, and we'd have a job getting out of this underground

place without their help. Let's only use our magic powers as a last resort."

"But what are we going to do then?" whined Coral.

"Let's not lose hope." Robin tried to comfort her as his mind raced. "The Korrigans are gamblers. I think I have an idea . . ."

The advancing Korrigans were about to place their little cats' paws on them when Robin announced his brainwave. He turned to Kor Mehtar,

"Lord of this realm, if you agree
we're willing to wager our liberty."

Kor Mehtar looked amusedly at the boy while the other Korrigans awaited the King's reply.

"It's a deal, I like your pluck
but don't expect to win on luck!"

These words were greeted with delighted applause. A Council meeting was called immediately around the throne and a heated argument ensued, apparently about the choice of game and the rules. The gang took advantage to go into a huddle.

"I'm certain it will work," said Robin triumphantly. "The Korrigans can never resist a challenge! I only hope they won't be too vicious if they win."

"Robin," queried Godfrey, "this 'somebody' the King was talking about who wants to get their hands on you — would that be The Shadow again?"

"Possibly," admitted Robin, trying to look unconcerned, so as not to worry his friends even more. "But the Korrigans are trustworthy. Well, usually. If we win at their game, I think they'll let us go."

"Why can't you use your Graphems to get us out of here?" asked Romaric.

"We're saving them in case of emergency," explained Bertram, instead of Robin. "It's a strategy Robin and I have agreed on, and which seems to me . . ."

"Oh, be quiet. Why don't you explain it to us in Korrigani?" taunted Amber, causing Bertram to give her a furious look.

"The beauty you mentioned, Robin," asked Coral, "was it me or was it Amber? Because being a star is OK, but it's not as nice as being called beautiful, and I think that . . ."

"Leave Robin alone," said Romaric angrily. "He did the best he could. You know how difficult it is to speak Korrigani. . . ."

"As far as I'm concerned," broke in Bertram, "you're the beautiful one, Coral, without a doubt!"

"Thank you Bertram! Lucky you're here." She laughed, flashing him a dazzling smile.

"Oh, stop arguing, everyone, for goodness' sake," said Godfrey.

Just then, Kor Mehtar signaled to them and a Korrigan nudged them toward the throne.

"Now the fun and games can start!
And all of you will take part.
My Council in its wisdom asks
that you complete certain tasks."

announced the King, smiling rather wickedly, Robin thought.

"Divide yourselves into teams of two
then I'll explain what you must do.
Two challenges await each pair

so you must choose who'll face which dare.
For the first you have to be very fit
while for the second you need brains and wit.
If the first fails, do not dismay
the other can still save the day."
But there was one thing that bothered Robin:
"Sire, I fear we're in a bit of a fix
there are seven of us, but three twos make six,"
To which Kor Mehtar replied:
"Robin, you will stay by me,
as you speak so fluently," with a hint of mischief in his voice.
Then the little men with their iron shoes and wagging tails led
Amber, Agatha, Coral, Godfrey, Romaric, and Bertram to the
center of the cavern. The Korrigans had assembled on the wooden
scaffolding that ran along the walls of the cave and were chattering and jumping up and down in excitement, making the most
indescribable racket.

"Try and concentrate," commanded Romaric. In the absence
of Robin, who had remained at the King's side, he had taken
charge. "Right, the King's decided to split us up. Too bad. So
let's divide into pairs: Amber, you go with Godfrey, Bertram
with Agatha, and Coral with me."

"Romaric! Am I the one who'll have to answer the questions?
Oh no, I'm scared," wailed Coral.

"Don't worry, Coral." Bertram tried to comfort her by tapping his bag. "If things get out of hand, I've got more than one
trick in my bag!"

"Does listening to your nonsense count as one of the trials?"

complained Amber. "Right, Godfrey, I'll do the trial and you answer the riddle."

"You're on," agreed Godfrey.

"So, sweet Agatha," began Bertram, turning to his partner. "And how are we going to divide the tasks? What a cruel dilemma! Would it be best for me to be the athlete or the brains? What do you think?"

"I don't know," replied Agatha with a shrug. "All I know is that I must be crazy to be so fond of that apprentice sorcerer who brings me nothing but bad luck! First of all, because of him, I was kidnapped by Gommons, and that horrid brute Thunku treated me like a slave for weeks. And now, here I am a prisoner of the Korrigans and forced to play some stupid game! If only I had a decent partner, who was capable of stringing three words together without talking complete nonsense . . ."

"OK, I'll let you answer the questions then," concluded Bertram sheepishly, as Amber, Godfrey, and Romaric smiled knowingly.

A Korrigan wearing a blue hat was walking over to them, puffing out his chest. Perched on his stone throne, Kor Mehtar was jubilant. The Korrigan in the blue hat bowed before the King, then addressed the young people:

"I've been appointed your referee,
so don't even think of crossing me."

"This isn't going to be easy," Amber murmured in Godfrey's ear.

"You masterminds, the game is now afoot,
Approach the throne while the others stay put!" announced the referee, gesticulating theatrically.

Coral, trembling from head to foot, Agatha, dragging her feet, and Godfrey, whistling nonchalantly, went up to the throne, beside which stood Robin.

"Be brave, Coral, you'll be fine," he whispered encouragingly, receiving a nervous smile in return.

The Korrigan who was acting as referee then turned to Amber, Romaric, and Bertram, who had been left alone in the center of the floor.

"So, now you must decide
which athlete from your lands,
is keen to triumph with their hands?"

"I'm the most dextrous," Bertram boasted to the others, waggling his fingers, "from handling the Graphems. . . ."

Amber and Romaric exchanged a dubious look, and gave in. In any case, they would all have to do something.

"OK, then go on . . ."

Bertram took a step forward.

"So this is the first conceited fool
who's bound to fail though he thinks he'll rule!"

The referee's commentary had the audience howling with laughter.

They're making fun of us, thought Robin, clenching his fists with rage. *I bet the games are rigged!*

As if to confirm Robin's suspicion, the referee explained to the horrified Bertram that he had to walk all the way around the cave on his hands, without overbalancing. Amber and Romaric were distraught; only Amber would have been capable of such a feat!

"Next round," muttered Amber, "we'd better think more carefully!"

Bertram shot his companions a look of pure panic.

Then he mentally steeled himself, "Bertram, you're going to fall flat on your face, but your honor is at stake! At least you have to try!"

Reluctantly, he put down his bag and removed his cloak. Then he placed his hands on the ground and kicked his legs in the air, trying to find his balance. When he finally succeeded, he set off along the sandy track.

"He has a certain courage," admitted Romaric.

"It's also called pride," Amber corrected him. "But you're right, the clumsy idiot has a loyal heart!"

Cheered on by his friends, Bertram managed to walk about ten feet before collapsing onto the ground, to the Korrigans' great delight.

"I'm sorry . . ." sighed Bertram to Amber and Romaric as he dusted himself off.

"You did your best," reassured Romaric with a friendly clap on the back.

"And it wasn't too bad," said Amber, flashing him a smile for the first time.

Then they turned toward the throne.

"*Who among you will use their loaf,*

to rescue the pride of this clumsy oaf?" asked the King, looking at Agatha.

"*That would be me,*

Your Majesty," replied Agatha, giving Kor Mehtar a look filled with scorn which was utterly lost on him.

"*Well you impudent girl,*

this will set your mind in a whirl:

My first is in pancake and also in crêpe
My second is in loaf as well as in roll
My third is in apple as well as in grape
My fourth is in buckwheat, but not in whole
My fifth is in chicken and also in broth
My sixth is in turkey and also in legs
My last is in dishrag but not in cloth
My whole is a way of preparing your eggs."

Agatha more or less understood Korrigani, like all the students of The Lost Isle, but Robin still translated the riddle to be certain she had grasped it. Agatha racked her brains.

It's easy! thought Robin. *I hope she's not going to get confused! Oh no, I'm going to have to help her. . . .*

With the utmost discretion, Robin traced a Mudra with his fingers, calling on the Torch Graphem, Kenaz, which stimulated creativity. Then he mentally sent it to Agatha.

Nothing happened. Agatha, still pondering the riddle, seemed to be completely flummoxed.

It looks as though Kenaz isn't working, thought Robin in disbelief. *Now what? I hope that doesn't mean that the Graphems don't work in Korrigan territory! That would be the last straw.*

The King was growing impatient:

"Why are we having to wait so long?
Could it be you think you'll get it wrong?"

"Oh dear," Agatha's brain felt scrambled, she just couldn't remember all the clues. But hold on, what was the last one? *My whole is a way of preparing your eggs* . . . scrambled brain . . . scrambled eggs! Luckily, she had the presence of mind to speak English, leaving it to Robin to translate her reply into Korrigani.

"*Your attempt at a riddle is easily foiled;*
poached is the answer, not scrambled or boiled," translated Robin, unperturbed, and hoping with all his heart that Kor Mehtar did not understand the language of The Lost Isle.

Agatha turned pale when she realized that she'd got it wrong, and that without Robin's intervention they would all have been lost. But she managed to remain composed under the King's suspicious scowl. The referee awaited a sign from Kor Mehtar. As soon as it came, he leaped once more into the center of the cave.

"*You may have won the first by a whisker*
but the second challenge will certainly be brisker!"

30

A TIGHT SPOT

The Korrigan in the blue hat was relishing the anxiety visible on Amber's and Romaric's faces. He continued:

"The next challenge you'll find is no mean feat,
so which of you is nimblest on their feet?"

"Let's take our time," warned Amber. "Let's think. What can he mean by nimble?"

"Is he going to make us hop? Juggle with a ball? Make us dance the can-can? How are we supposed to know?" snapped Romaric tensely.

While Amber and Romaric tried to work out what they might be asked to do before making up their minds who would attempt the second trial, Agatha, by the throne, was being comforted by the others. Coral confessed that she wouldn't have got the right answer, and Godfrey praised her for having had the presence of mind to answer in English.

"I was so nervous," Agatha reproached herself. "I couldn't concentrate and I forgot half the clues. . . . In any case, thanks for saving me once again," she declared, throwing her arms around Robin's neck and kissing him on both cheeks.

Robin wriggled free from Agatha's embrace and glanced over at Amber, but she was absorbed in her discussion with Romaric, and hadn't witnessed the scene. Coral pretended to look elsewhere, and Godfrey stifled an urge to burst out laughing.

Just then, Amber started walking toward the Korrigan in the blue hat. All eyes were on her. Rubbing his hands together, the referee explained what lay in store for her: She was to do forty skips with a skipping rope! Romaric sighed with relief. They'd made the right decision after all.

Two Korrigans stepped forward with a skipping rope. They each took an end and began to turn it.

Amber closed her eyes. She had been the skipping champion at primary school; she should still be able to do it! She reopened them, steadied her breathing and went up to the rope and jumped in.

"One, two, three, four . . ." counted her friends out loud. "Eleven, twelve, thirteen, fourteen . . ."

Amber jumped nimbly. She was completely focused. The referee pulled a face and glanced at the King who looked furious. He made a discreet sign to the two Korrigans turning the rope and they suddenly began to turn it much faster.

"That's . . . not . . . fair. . . ." panted Amber.

"Thirty-one, thirty-two, thirty-three, thirty . . . Ohhhhhh!"

The rope had tripped her up and knocked her to the floor, amid the joyous shouts of the Korrigans who, in their excitement, were shaking the walkways and platforms onto which they were crowded.

"But . . . they're cheating!" exclaimed Coral, red with indignation.

"Of course they're cheating," said Godfrey with a sigh, advancing toward the King. "My turn now. I hope I'm up to it!"

Romaric had rushed over to help Amber to her feet. She was livid. They both looked in the direction of the throne.

The King had called over a young Korrigan, and was whispering instructions in his ear. The young Korrigan then went over to Robin with a big smile, and politely raised his huge hat:

"Hello! My name be Kor Hosik! I understanding your Lost Isle language! My King asking me to listen to what you say! My King afraid you cheating!"

"Oh, he is, is he?" retorted Agatha.

"Very good, Kor Hosik. I'm pleased to meet you," was all Robin could reply, hoping desperately that Godfrey would answer the King's question correctly, and even more fervently, after a glance in Coral's direction, that Romaric would succeed in the third physical trial.

Without further ado, Kor Mehtar fired a riddle at Godfrey:

"My first is in tea but not in leaf
My second is in teapot and also in teeth
My third is in caddy but not in cosy
My fourth is in cup but not in rosy
My fifth is in herbal and also in health
My sixth is in peppermint and always in wealth
My last is in drink, so what can I be?
I'm there in a classroom, are you listening to me?"

Robin carefully translated the teaser while Kor Hosik watched him and listened closely.

At first, Godfrey panicked, it sounded very complicated . . . peppermint, wealth . . . something to do with tea, no doubt, but then he realized that the King was trying to confuse him and that last line actually gave it all away. So, after a moment's thought, he calmly replied,

"Caddy, peppermint, that's all rot.
The answer is teacher, is it not?"

Kor Mehtar stamped his foot with rage, while Agatha, Coral, and Robin clapped their friend on the back.

The Korrigan in the blue hat, who was no longer laughing, rushed over to Romaric and hissed spitefully:

"Well, boy, the last challenge is yours
but you're no match for my strong paws.
And no one can equal my splendid muscles
so I'm unbeaten in arm-wrestling tussles!"

Some Korrigans brought a table and two low chairs. Romaric sat on one, and the Korrigan in the blue hat sat facing him.

"A referee taking part in his own game, that takes the cake," Amber scowled.

"If I may be so bold," replied Bertram, "the gnome in the blue hat has been biased from the start!"

"You're right," she agreed. "I hope Romaric will teach him a lesson!"

"Alas, I fear he won't," said Bertram with a genuine sigh of regret.

The Korrigan placed his elbow on the table and presented the palm of his pawlike hand to Romaric, who suppressed a shudder as he clasped it.

"Well, shall we begin,

before my patience wears thin?"

Romaric replied defiantly,

"You'll really be a gnome with the blues
when it's me who makes you lose!"

His opponent glowered at him and the trial of strength began.

Romaric soon realized that despite his size, his opponent was much stronger than him. However, he decided to put up the best fight he could.

The feel of the little hairy claw against his palm did not help his concentration. He resisted for as long as he could, then, exhausted, he surrendered as his opponent forced the back of his hand onto the table.

The audience cheered wildly and the triumphant Korrigan threw his hat up into the air.

"Oh no, it's my turn now!" wailed Coral. "Can I give my turn to someone else?"

"Hardly, seeing as you're last." Agatha sighed.

"You'll do it, I know you will," Robin tried to reassure her as she walked toward the throne. "Didn't you get the better of those jellyfish in the Infested Sea?"

"Yes," breathed Coral. "But this is different — it all depends on me now!"

"Romaric's life also depended on you in The Uncertain World, and you saved him. I know you can do it. . . ."

"Thank you, Robin," said Coral shakily, before kissing him on the cheek.

"Another one who wants to kiss you," whispered Godfrey. "You must tell me your secret! I'll sell it to Bertram for a fortune. . . ."

"Can't you be serious for five minutes?"

"Yes, but only when I'm playing music. And even then, maybe not for five minutes . . ."

Kor Mehtar, having watched with amusement Coral's growing anxiety, finally asked her the question:

My first is in playfellow, also in fun
My second's in race and also in run.
My third is in smile, in kind, and in like
My fourth is in game, in ride, and in bike.
My fifth is in plan, but it isn't in play
My last is in shared, in enjoyed, and in day."

Robin translated the riddle and looked questioningly at Coral, who had shut her eyes so as to concentrate. Romaric, Bertram, and Amber waited apprehensively.

"If she says only one clever thing in her life, let this be the time," murmured Amber.

The King was trembling with impatience on his throne. He interrupted Coral's train of thought in a triumphant voice:

"The puzzle I set was really tough
but I think you've had long enough!"

Coral opened her eyes and saw her friends all smiling encouragement. The answer was . . . her friends . . . of course!

She beamed at the King and answered in perfect Korrigani,

"At last our trials are at an end —
The answer you're looking for is friend!"

The cave echoed with cries and groans. The King let out a howl of rage, while the referee rolled on the ground and began to eat his hat. Amber barged past the others and raced over to Coral to hug and congratulate her.

"How did you do it so fast?" she asked admiringly.

"I don't know," confessed Coral awkwardly. "Everything suddenly felt easy, even Korrigani, which I normally find horribly difficult to speak!"

"How do you explain that, Robin?" asked Romaric, bursting with pride at Coral's achievement.

"I think that Coral isn't nearly as stupid as you think," Robin grinned evasively.

The apprentice knew exactly what had happened: Kenaz, the Graphem that stimulates the brain, which he had invoked to help Agatha, had had a delayed action and worked on Coral instead. Here was another mystery to be solved!

"In The Uncertain World," he said to himself, "where the sky isn't the same as that of The Lost Isle, the Graphems and their powers are different. But here, we're still on The Lost Isle! Does being underground weaken the Graphems? Do the Korrigans possess spells capable of blocking ours?"

Experience had taught him that it was best to keep one step ahead. Now was the time to act, whatever the risk. Taking advantage of the general commotion, Robin mentally constructed a complex Galdr and, with the help of a Mudra, discreetly sent it into the center of the cave. As he expected, nothing happened. Now his friends were pushing him toward the throne.

"Go on, ask him to release us now," demanded Amber. "This has gone beyond a joke."

Robin bowed before the King of the Korrigans.

"Sire, we've solved all the riddles you set
and now it's time to honor your debt."

The King wrung his hands and groaned.

"Alas, young Robin, I'd like to say yes
for I've been amazed by your prowess.
You've earned your freedom, but I lied
I can't let you go, my hands are tied.
He who has more power than a king,
has claim on you and I can't do a thing."

"What? But that's cheating!" fumed Coral.

"You have no right!" shouted Agatha.

"I thought Korrigans had more honor than that," said Godfrey contemptuously.

Kor Mehtar, unmoved by their outraged protests, motioned for them to be led away to prison.

Bertram slid his hand inside his bag, as if looking for something. Robin caught him and shot him an inquiring look. The sorcerer blushed guiltily and quickly withdrew his hand.

"Right," he whispered in Robin's ear, "you'll see what a sorcerer can do when his friends are in danger!"

Bertram raised his arm and assumed a terrifying expression.

31

BETTER LATE THAN NEVER

"You never prosper when you cheat,
  so all your gods you'd better entreat
or failing that, be quick on your feet
  to escape the spells that I complete!" cried Bertram in clumsy
Korrigani, more theatrical than ever.

Before Robin could step in, his friend executed a series of
Stadha while chanting a spell calling down the winds to sweep
away the Korrigans, lightning to destroy the cave, and the earth
to open up to allow the friends to reach the surface. Lastly,
Bertram wove his Galdr and froze in a pose that was both menacing and triumphant — and at the same time a bit stupid.

But nothing happened at all.

The sorcerer was bewildered, and glanced panic-stricken
at Robin, who could do nothing but shake his head and shrug
helplessly.

The assembled Korrigans burst out laughing and the King
seemed to find his good humor again.

"*The Lost Isle's magic possesses cruel charms,*" Kor Mehtar beamed at the disconcerted sorcerer.

"*But you need to do more than wave your arms!*
Still, let me set your mind at rest
Your technique is fine, you did your best.
Korrigan magic is ancient and twofold
Your magic is single, yet not very old.
Ours comes from the moon and the earth, our home
Yours is from the stars in heaven's dome.
Arcane Graphems assure your powers
Red earthy Oghams are the source of ours.
That's all I'll say — I've told you far too much
Your tricks won't work here, however deft your touch!"

The Korrigans who had been ordered to take them away and lock them up closed in on them once again.

It's still too soon for the delayed spell, thought Robin. *It would be disastrous if they took us out of the cavern now. . . . We must play for time!*

"O, Korrigan King, who is so kind and just," he cried to cover his confusion,

"*You owe us something as you betrayed our trust*
Most royal prisoners get one last request
and we should be treated just like all the rest. . . ."

Kor Mehtar looked thoughtful, then replied,

"*What can be the desire of one so young*
Robin, the sorcerer with the silver tongue?
Tell me what you want and I will say
if I can grant it before you're locked away."

Robin stood before the King with folded arms and pleaded,

*"Korrigan magic fills us with great awe
and we'd be interested in learning more
about powers that form such ancient lore. . . ."*

The King said nothing, but summoned Kor Hosik, the Korrigan interpreter, and whispered in his ear.

"Cousin," said Romaric in amazement, "I know you're dedicated, but do you think this is the time to be taking an interest in the Korrigans' sorcery?"

"I know what I'm doing," replied Robin, determined to take advantage of Kor Hosik's absence to let his friends know what he was up to. "Listen, in a few minutes, something should happen that's going to create chaos in the cave. Be ready to follow me. . . ."

"What's going to happen?" asked Coral.

"Don't tell us," Amber butted in. "Bertram's going to take his clothes off and do a belly dance in the middle of the floor!"

"Very funny!" said Bertram huffily.

"Oh, go on," added Godfrey, "not everybody has such a gift for comedy!"

"Leave him alone," said Coral defensively. "He did his best to get us out of this mess!"

"That's the problem," snapped Agatha. "He always does his best and it's never up to very much."

"Shut up," warned Robin. "Kor Hosik's coming back."

The Korrigan was walking toward them with a broad smile. He bowed and spoke to them haltingly in their own language.

"My King agreeing to talk to you about our Oghams. He choosing me to speak, so like that you all understanding. And because me not know many things, so me can't betray secrets!

Oghams be Korrigans' magic signs. Each Ogham having plant name, because leaves illuminated by moon and roots nourished from earth. Plant is link between things on surface and things inside. Oghams painted red because earth and moon connected by blood ties. Long ago, men also loving Oghams. Then other men coming on the sea, with other magic hidden in stars, and men forget Oghams. There, me not know any more. Me still too young! Only one hundred and sixty years old!"

"He certainly looks good for his age," remarked Godfrey drily.

"Thank you," replied the Korrigan, seemingly delighted.

Kor Hosik turned to the King and indicated that he had finished. The King immediately gave the order for the young people to be seized and led away.

"Now," said Robin between clenched teeth. "Now . . . please, wretched Galdr, act now . . ."

As if in answer to his prayers, there was suddenly a tremendous commotion in the spot where, a little while earlier, Robin had cast his spell.

A starry spiral burst from the ground, grew, and began to whirl. Then it exploded and scattered a shower of tiny stars all over the cave.

There was pandemonium. The Korrigans dropped down onto the ground from their platforms and rushed around in all directions, shrieking in terror.

Kor Mehtar stood on his throne and began to dance his ritual magic, making elaborate signs with his arms and hands:

"Cweorth! Tumult of the storm that rages
crusher of the ice of ages

By the power of night's dark eye,
let the roaring gales draw nigh
and make this spinning fire die!"

There were showers of red sparks where Kor Mehtar's magic collided with Robin's Galdr. But the spell held good, to the King's astonishment.

"The sorcerer who cast this charm
is strong enough to do us harm!
This is the first time that this lore
has been unleashed at our very core!
Tremble, youngsters, for your shenanigans,
have made an enemy of the Korrigans!"

Kor Mehtar turned to the gang, who hadn't moved, and started his invocations again.

"Why don't we just get out of here?" moaned Coral.

"Not yet," replied Robin. "Wait for my signal!"

The Korrigan King was dancing frenziedly, gesticulating and chanting:

"Eyar! Veiled traveler of night's terrain,
orb that hangs in heaven's domain.
By the power of the moonlit moor,
and he who groans before death's door,
bury these uplanders for ever more!"

The Ogham invoked by the King appeared before them in a red flash. But before it engulfed them, it was halted by the glowing dust of the exploded Graphems. Kor Mehtar choked with rage.

"Now!" yelled Robin, grabbing a jar of glowworms and dragging his friends after him.

They raced down the passage that smelled of moldy earth which they had come down earlier. The Korrigans instantly jumped up to follow them. But they suddenly felt their legs grow heavy and their movements become sluggish. . . .

"Robin! How did you do that?" asked Bertram, open-mouthed in amazement.

He was walking, doubled over, behind the apprentice, as they made their way down the narrow passage.

"The first time I cast a spell," replied Robin, "I noticed it had a delayed effect. So, when I sensed that the situation was turning nasty, I prepared a Galdr in advance. . . ."

"Genius, absolute genius!" enthused Bertram. "And what did you put in it?"

"Naudhiz, which neutralized Kor Mehtar's first magic attack. And then Yera, the Rejected, the Graphem of the Cycle, which slowed down the second attack. And lastly Dagaz, which suspends time, to hold them back."

"You foresaw all that?" asked Bertram, stunned.

"Well, it makes sense," explained Robin. "With the delayed effect combined with the magic of the Korrigans in the cavern, I knew that my three Graphems would work one after the other. I was certain that the King would try and destroy my Galdr, and that then he'd try and attack us with his magic before thinking of using physical means. . . ."

"Robin, Robin, I'm in awe of you!" gushed Bertram. "You are my hero, my master, I'll serve you forever!"

"Hmm . . . don't you think that's going a bit far? Supposing I took you at your word — you'd find that a bit tough."

"You're such a smart apprentice," went on Bertram as if he hadn't heard a word. "Tell me, why did the Galdr explode?"

"I have no idea," confessed Robin. "Perhaps as a reaction to the Korrigans' magic. In any case, it didn't affect the power of my spell. On the contrary, it strengthened it!"

"Speak up a bit, will you? We can't hear anything you're saying!" shouted Amber behind them.

"It's none of your business," replied Bertram, turning around. "It's a top secret conversation between members of the Guild, and —"

"Silence!" Robin suddenly shouted. "We have a problem. . . ."

All six gathered around the apprentice. The glowworms in their jar illuminated three tunnels leading in different directions.

"Does anybody remember which passage we came down?" asked Robin.

32
THE NIGHT BEFORE COMBAT

Urian, armed to the teeth, was pacing up and down the vast dining room of Penmarch Castle. He stopped in front of the fireplace, above which the Penmarch family coat of arms was proudly displayed: a white bird flying over a black landscape, against a red sky.

The giant felt emotional. How many times had he taken courage from these ancestral colors before one of those impossible quests where men find their self respect and purpose? Urian felt alive again!

"Valentino!" he bellowed.

"Already here, old comrade," Valentino greeted him cheerfully, putting down the bags he'd packed.

"By Jove, my friend!" replied Urian with a huge guffaw, "I was afraid you'd leave without me!"

"You look magnificent in your armor," said Valentino loyally.

"Do you think so?" said Urian. "Bah! What's armor compared to this!"

Urian took out a hatchet from its sheath and whirled it above his head.

"You're such a boy at heart!" Valentino teased him gently.

In truth, he felt just as excited.

"Isn't Quadehar coming?" inquired Urian, putting his hatchet away.

"He's resting. He'll join us later. He thinks it's best to arrive in The Uncertain World in the dead of night."

Urian groaned with impatience, but soon calmed down. The lull before battle had a particular quality that he relished.

He threw a bundle of wood into the hearth, then brought over two stools and placed them by the fireside. Then he sat down next to Valentino. Soon, the two men were talking animatedly as they relived their past exploits.

≈ ✳ ≈ ✳ ≈

"Are you ready?" asked Quadehar, bursting into the room.

Urian and Valentino jumped. Most of the night had slipped away, and they had long stopped talking, their gaze absorbed by the dancing flames and their own thoughts. Each man was lost in his own personal memories, especially those times when they had looked death in the face.

"We're ready, Quadehar," replied Urian. "By Jove, we're ready all right!"

"Pick up your things then. We're off."

The sorcerer led the two knights into the center of the dining room, where they shouldered the bags that Valentino had packed.

"There's only one thing that bothers me," complained Urian. "And that's having to travel without a horse!"

"I'm sorry," explained Quadehar, "but horses can't cope with the journey between the Worlds. Now, concentrate, and try to copy every one of my movements as accurately as possible. The Desert Galdr requires careful concentration."

"Yes, you've already told us all that," Urian broke in irritably.

"If I'm telling you again, it's because I know what we're up against," snapped Quadehar, glaring at the giant.

Urian hung his head and bit his lip.

"Come on, Urian," Valentino urged gently, "don't be foolish. . . ."

"Right, are you ready?" asked Quadehar impatiently. "We're not going to remain here for the rest of the night, I hope!"

Urian meekly took the sorcerer's hand and held the other one out to his friend.

Quadehar adopted the successive postures of the eight Graphems that made up the Galdr, muttering the spell.

The knights imitated him as best they could.

Suddenly, they heard a door open, then slam shut, and they were sucked into a powerful whirlwind and hurled into a black vortex.

The three men had left The Lost Isle.

≋ ✳ ≋ ✳ ≋

The Shadow was pacing up and down in his stone tower. The nebulous form seemed to be tormented by a terrible anxiety. In his agitation, shreds of darkness broke off and faded into the walls with a sizzling sound.

"So why are they taking so long . . . to bring me the child? I warned all those who revere me or fear me . . . that I wanted the child at once. . . . at once . . . that I'd pay the price. . . . Do I have to do everything myself? Useless, every single one of them . . . useless . . . I'm surrounded by imbeciles. . . ."

The sound of hurried footsteps could be heard on the stairs. The Shadow turned and stared at the door. A breathless Lomgo appeared.

"A message, Master, from The Lost Isle."

"Well, what are you waiting for, faithful scribe? Read it, read me the message . . . and pray that it's good news. . . ."

Lomgo recovered his breath. Then, after darting an anxious glance at the figure who seemed to be trembling beneath his cloak of shadow, he slowly read:

"Grim Lord in your somber tower
before whose wrath we all must cower
your wait is over, so be of good cheer —
the boy you sought is with me here.
Inform me of the place and hour
so I can deliver him into your power.
Your humble servant from afar,
the Korrigan King, Kor Mehtar."

"The Korrigans . . . the Korrigans found him first. . . . Curse those gnomes and their impertinence. . . . They'll pay for this . . . one day . . . but the main thing, yes, the main thing . . . is that the boy shall be mine . . . mine. . . ."

The Shadow let out a demented laugh and the scribe made a hasty exit.

33

THE ESCAPE

Stumped, Robin and his friends considered the three corridors facing them.

"I think we arrived from the one on the right," declared Godfrey.

"Really?" replied Agatha. "I could have sworn it was the one on the left."

"We'll have to rely on the Graphems once again!" Robin sighed.

"The problem is," objected Bertram with a frown, "that it's likely to take a while before they respond."

"I know," replied Robin. "But, yet again, we have no option. . . ."

The apprentice closed his eyes and called up Perthro, the Dice Cup, which the sorcerers often used as a guide through the maze-like paths of the Wyrd. He whispered its name. As predicted, the Graphem did not appear.

"Let's hope that Perthro gets here before the Korrigans catch up with us," was all Robin could say, as he slumped on the floor. The others joined him.

"Let's play a game while we're waiting," suggested Coral.

The others simply stared at her in disbelief. Even Romaric reprimanded her.

"Keep your hair on, I was just joking," Coral grinned.

"Well, I for one," remarked Amber, changing the subject, "think we've done very well, so far."

"It's true," agreed Romaric. "We're the real champions!"

"And if the Korrigans hadn't cheated us," added Godfrey, "we'd have left with a bag of gold coins!"

"Yes, my friends, everything went very well," agreed Bertram solemnly. "Unfortunately, I failed. . . . But luckily, Agatha was there to make up for my pathetic performance!"

"Oh, come on, Bertram!" Romaric consoled him. "I wasn't much better! The only one who might have passed her test was Amber, if the Korrigans hadn't double-crossed her."

"As for my answer," broke in Agatha sheepishly, "I'm embarrassed just thinking about it. If Robin hadn't been there . . ."

"We've all got Robin to thank for saving our skins!" exclaimed Godfrey.

"I absolutely agree!" enthused Bertram. "I propose a round of applause for our hero!"

"Hmm . . . but not too loud, OK?" replied Robin, blushing slightly. "We don't want the Korrigans —"

"Three cheers for our savior!" went on Bertram, taking no notice. "Hip hip . . . !"

"Hooray!" they chorused.

"Hip hip . . . !"

"Hooray!"

Robin suddenly raised his hand to request silence, closed his eyes, and concentrated.

"Great," he announced. "Perthro's appeared! It's the middle corridor, without question."

Godfrey and Agatha, who were convinced it was one of the other two, exchanged sheepish looks.

"Quick!" ordered Romaric. "The Korrigans are probably already on our trail."

The friends ran down the passage at once, moving as fast as they could. They soon came to another fork but, guided by the Graphem, they knew which corridor to take.

At last they came to the foot of the staircase leading up to the dolmen. The exit had been left open and they raced up the stone steps four at a time.

"Whew!" exclaimed Amber, gulping in the fragrant night air. "I would never have thought that one day I'd be so desperate for fresh air!"

"I'm just happy to see the stars again," confessed Robin, glancing in Bertram's direction. It would be a relief to both of them to know the Graphems would respond normally in sight of the stars of The Lost Isle.

"Sorry to be a killjoy," announced Romaric, "but we'd better not hang around here. I can hear shouting from under-ground. . . ."

"You're right," said Robin. "Let's go!"

They set off over the moor in the direction of Dashtikazar.

"Can Korrigans run fast?" asked Coral anxiously.

"About twice as fast as humans," replied Bertram.

"Do you think we'll get to Dashtikazar before they catch up with us?"

"Not if it really was them that Romaric heard earlier."

"Let's get a move on, then!" urged Agatha, glancing apprehensively over her shoulder.

Behind them, the moor rustled with the sounds of a thousand footsteps.

The seven friends broke into a run amid the heather and bushes, frightened by the strange shadows cast on the ground by the moon.

"Faster! Faster!" yelled Romaric, who had hung back to encourage the girls trailing behind.

Coral screamed. She had bumped into Agatha and the two of them went rolling on the ground. Romaric raced over to help them up.

The others stopped in their tracks.

"What do we do?" asked Bertram, addressing Robin.

"We're done for!" wailed Godfrey. "The Korrigans are hot on our heels. . . ."

Just then, out of nowhere, hundreds of cats' paws grabbed at the fugitives' legs and arms. Within moments, the seven friends found themselves captive once more.

34

STRONGER THAN MAGIC

"What you do! What you do!" moaned Kor Hosik, the young Korrigan at the head of the pursuers. "Now King very angry!"

The captives were made to stand in a line. This time, the Korrigans did not even tie them up, they were so sure of themselves.

To the strange call of a horn hollowed out from a dried root, Kor Mehtar appeared in a sedan chair borne on the shoulders of six Korrigans. As soon as it was placed on the ground, the King leaped out and executed a pirouette.

"You've angered and insulted me,
with such a foolish attempt to flee!
I'll be avenged and make you pay
for the insult I've suffered today!"

He really did look furious, and kept turning somersaults while he spoke.

"We are truly sorry,

Your high Maj —" Robin tried to explain before the King cut him short, raising a menacing hand in his direction.

"Silence, boy! Button your lip!
It's lucky you're taking a little trip.
So I can't punish you for your insolence
but I guarantee you'll soon see sense!"

Kor Mehtar signaled to two Korrigans to seize Robin.

"The only one I want is you,
so you can bid your friends adieu.
They'll rot away in a Korrigan cell
till icicles hang from the roof of hell!
As for you, so long as you draw breath,
you'll suffer a fate that's worse than death!"

Robin turned pale. The others felt their legs turn to jelly. The Korrigans greeted the King's announcement with shouts of glee. They began to rush at Coral, Agatha, Bertram, Godfrey, Amber, and Romaric.

"And don't think of calling on the stars,
or your six friends will bear the scars!"

Kor Mehtar threatened, his somber gaze boring into Robin's green eyes. This was no practical joke. This was deadly serious.

Then the King marched back to his sedan chair. The two Korrigans who were keeping a firm grip on Robin dragged him toward the moor.

"Robin! No!" screamed Amber, struggling to free herself.

"Shh, Amber." Romaric tried to calm her. "There's nothing you can do."

But Amber had gone berserk and was thrashing around wildly.

Her eyes rolled upward until only the whites were visible. A terrifying strangled groan escaped from her throat.

"Amber! What's the matter?" said a panicked Romaric.

"I promise you, nothing happened in Robin's room in Penmarch!" exclaimed Agatha, terrified.

But Amber was obsessed with a much more serious mission. Oblivious to her friends' anxious efforts to calm her down, she had eyes only for Robin, who was being dragged away. All of a sudden, as if driven by a superhuman strength, she swept aside the Korrigan who was holding her arms, sending him flying. Then she gave the one who was holding onto her legs such a violent thump that he was knocked out and, with a glazed expression, she headed straight for Robin and his kidnappers.

A Korrigan tried to stop her, but soon regretted it, as Amber grabbed him by the throat and flung him into a bush.

A ripple of panic went through the column of Korrigans.

"Wow! Does she do this often?" asked Bertram, his eyes wide in disbelief.

"I think this is the first time," replied Romaric.

"I . . . I swear," stammered Agatha gulping, "and I give you all my solemn promise that I'll never cross her path again!"

"It's just like her to whack a Korrigan," remarked Coral, "but I had no idea she was that strong!"

"A Hamingja," murmured Bertram.

"What did you say?" asked Romaric.

"I said that there's something unnatural about her behavior and that there's only one possible explanation: She's been bewitched."

"What do you mean?"

"It's a thing of the past," went on Bertram. "People were conditioned to react in a certain way in certain circumstances by a spell that had been imprinted on them, unbeknownst to them! They were Hamingjas. But nowadays, such practices are banned."

"Are you saying somebody's put a spell on my sister?" cried Coral. "But you're wrong! You really have no romance in you, Bertram, can't you see that it's love that gives her superhuman powers?"

"In my opinion," said Godfrey, looking doubtful, "Amber's taken leave of her senses. She obviously can't bear to see Robin taken away. Everybody knows that mad people are much stronger than normal people."

"Think what you like," grumbled Bertram, upset that nobody was prepared to listen to him. "I see what I see and I know what I know. . . ."

Meanwhile, Kor Mehtar had climbed on top of the sedan chair and was dancing up and down to invoke the power of an Ogham. He projected it onto Amber, who was still advancing toward Robin, as if in a trance. The Ogham struck Amber with a shower of red sparks, and she crumpled onto the ground.

"Amber!" screamed Romaric.

"I'm getting tired of your circus tricks," hissed Kor Mehtar.
"Your failed escapes and your pyrotechnics.
Seize them, my Korrigans, right away,
catch these miscreants without delay!"

Heedless of Kor Mehtar's threats, Coral raced after her sister. Amber lay unconscious, but did not look hurt. Coral gently stroked her sister's hair and could not hold back a tear that rolled down her cheek. What had possessed her to make her run to help

Robin? Was she so desperately in love with him? Coral felt a pang of jealousy. What about her, when would she truly fall madly in love like this? Would that idiot Romaric ever admit his feelings for her so that her own could blossom?

Coral was brutally dragged away from Amber by two Korrigans. She tried to struggle, but one of her attackers slapped her hard. Romaric roared with anger and tried to come to her aid, but he was immediately overcome. Agatha and Godfrey groaned helplessly. The situation was completely out of hand.

"This is too much," Bertram said to himself. "Bertram, this time you must forget your sorcerer's pride and do something practical! It's the only solution, even if it isn't very nice. Or very legal . . . eating disgusting food, OK, playing their stupid games, maybe, but this time they've really overstepped the mark. You don't hit girls."

He mustered all his courage, took a deep breath, and plunged a trembling hand into his sorcerer's bag. He brought out a strange, small metal object which he pointed at the King.

There was a general shriek of horror. The Korrigans looked on in terror as the young sorcerer threatened Kor Mehtar with the mysterious object.

"*You know full well that those things are banned,*
how can you be so reckless and underhand?" protested the King, hopping from one foot to the other.

"*Great King, you'd better take my advice*," replied Bertram taking a step toward him,

"*and listen well for I won't say it twice.*
Call off your ankle-biting gnomes
and let my friends go to their homes,

and if you want to save your skin,
go back to your burrow with your kin!"

"What is it?" asked Godfrey, who couldn't identify the object Bertram was brandishing.

"I think it's a . . . gun!" breathed Romaric round-eyed. "In any case, that's what it looks like!"

"But guns are prohibited on The Lost Isle!" said Coral indignantly. "*No firearms in our land*, it's one of the most important laws."

"True," said Agatha, "but the Korrigans seem pretty rattled, so it's fine with me!"

Standing on the roof of his sedan chair, Kor Mehtar seemed deeply distressed.

In response to the King's indecision, Bertram challenged him again in his stuttering Korrigani:

"Well, noble Sire, have you made up your mind?
The right course of action isn't so hard to find.
Don't argue with me for the sake of pride
but let us go and save your hide!"

Watched by the speechless crowd of Korrigans and his friends, Bertram fired a shot in the air, as if he'd been doing it all his life. A gasp of horror rose up from the moor. Bertram cocked the gun again and pointed it at the King and his henchmen. Then he turned to Kor Hosik, the interpreter:

"I'm fed up with speaking your complicated language. Tell the King that he'd better let us go. Otherwise, I shall have no hesitation in firing the gun again. And that will be the end of him."

The Korrigan translated Bertram's words. The King contemplated the group of friends who had been challenging him almost since he'd set eyes on them. Then he issued a series of orders. The Korrigans immediately scattered over the moor, and Robin's captors abandoned him, still bound hand and foot, on the ground. Kor Mehtar installed himself in his sedan, whispered a few words to Kor Hosik, then left as fast as his bearers' legs would carry him.

"My King very tired," explained the interpreter. "You indeed very strong and possess secret weapon. And now dawn coming, and Korrigans no like sun . . ."

To the east, the horizon was beginning to grow pale, and the houses of Dashtikazar could just be seen in the distance.

Before setting off on the heels of the King, Kor Hosik turned around one more time and waved his hat at them:

"See you, see you!"

"I hope not," grunted Godfrey.

The grasses and bushes quivered one last time. Then, all was still. As if the friends had suddenly awoken from a bad dream, they found themselves alone on the moor.

Agatha and Godfrey went to untie Robin's bonds and remove the gag from over his mouth. As dawn broke, the gang gathered around Amber's unconscious body, waiting for her to come to, so that they could share the huge sense of relief at their escape. The friends had survived, but now they must get to safety as soon as possible.

35

BERTRAM'S SECRET

The gang, with Agatha and Coral at the head, followed by Romaric and Godfrey supporting Amber — who was still slowly coming to — and with Robin and Bertram bringing up the rear, reached Dashtikazar as the sun's first rays struck the moor.

The streets were deserted, but that was not unusual on the day after a holiday. They made their way through the empty city to Utigern Krakal's apartment without meeting a soul.

They barricaded themselves inside and collapsed onto the living room floor.

"I'm absolutely shattered!" said Godfrey, lying on his back.

"Me, too," admitted Coral. "I think I could sleep for a week!"

"Amber, how are you feeling?" asked Robin, squeezing her hand.

Amber managed a weak smile.

"I feel much better now."

"You gave us such a fright!" said Romaric. "Even so . . .

whatever possessed you to knock out the Korrigans and show such determination to get to Robin?"

"I . . . I don't know," confessed Amber, looking embarrassed. "I can't remember a thing."

"That's typical of an enchantment," repeated Bertram. "But you won't believe me!"

"An enchantment?" queried Robin.

"Bertram thinks that Amber's been bewitched and that's why she went absolutely crazy when she saw you being carried off by the two Korrigans," explained Godfrey.

"She has all the symptoms," continued Bertram, "rolling her eyes, trancelike movements, loss of memory, and headaches . . ."

"A spell," mused Robin. "Why not . . . but hang on, it doesn't add up! First of all, who would have put a spell on her? And when? And why?"

"Whatever," muttered Bertram. "I'm not forcing anyone to believe me! You're free to put your friend's weird behavior down to love or madness. . . ."

"How come you know so much about enchantments?" asked Coral suspiciously.

"My dear Coral," replied Bertram with a hint of smugness in his voice, "may I remind you that I am a sorcerer!"

"And the gun, is that part of the sorcerer's usual bag of tricks?" retorted Romaric curtly.

The squire's question made everyone uneasy. There was a heavy silence. All eyes were on Bertram. He looked defiant and folded his arms.

Robin went over to him and placed his hand on his shoulder, as a sign of affection.

"Bertram," he said quietly, "it might not be obvious, but we really are your friends. You and I pledged the symbols of friendship which you yourself drew on our hands with charcoal! Everybody here is fond of you. Even Romaric, beneath his gruff exterior. Godfrey too, despite his dreaminess. And Amber, believe it or not. She isn't always such a shrew. . . ."

"Me too, I'm very fond of you," Coral added hastily.

"You see, Coral as well," continued Robin while Romaric glowered at her. "Honestly, I know it's true. However, friendship is based on one vital element, and that is trust. So remember, it's give and take!"

Bertram looked Robin in the eyes and then gave in.

"All right. I'm going to trust you, because I haven't got enough friends to be able to afford to lose any! My story isn't very long, and it's rather sad. . . ."

He was silent for a moment.

Facing him, his friends, despite their exhaustion, waited attentively for him to speak.

"Once, Robin," he began, "you remarked on my accent and you asked me where I came from, do you remember? I told you that I was from Jaggar, the little village in the Golden Mountains that was destroyed by The Shadow's army. . . ."

"Yes, I remember," replied Robin.

"That was to stop you from asking any more awkward questions. The truth is, I was born in The Real World!"

If a Gommon had burst into the room at that moment, it would have been less of a shock to the friends.

"What do you mean, you were born in The Real World?"

asked Robin. "You do mean The Real World that lies beyond The First Door?"

"Yes," confirmed Bertram. "I was born there and I lived there until I was eleven. Which explains my accent, and the fact that I sometimes seem like an outsider. There are some habits that are hard to shake off. . . ."

"Do all the children in The Real World carry guns?" asked Romaric.

"Of course not! My father was a soldier and he was issued a gun. When I was very young he taught me to be wary of it, but he also showed me how to use it. . . ."

"You used the past tense," Agatha pointed out. "Is your father . . . dead?"

"Both my parents died in a car crash," confided Bertram in a flat voice.

"*What* a sad story," said Coral softly.

"But how did you end up on The Lost Isle?" asked Godfrey in amazement. "Wow. This is the first time I've heard of somebody being permitted to come from The Real World to The Lost Isle!"

"My case is a little unusual," admitted Bertram. "In fact, my father was a Renouncer . . . Like yours, Robin, I believe! And his dream was to become a knight, just like you, Romaric! He was accepted into the Brotherhood as a squire, but he didn't succeed in becoming a fully fledged knight. He was bitterly disappointed. That's why he left The Lost Isle, and became a soldier in The Real World, where he met my mother. When I became an orphan, my godfather, who was my father's school friend, obtained special authorization to bring me to The Lost Isle and look after me. I smuggled the gun in with me, as a memento of my child-hood in The Real World. I discovered firearms were banned here and hid it. Nobody ever found out."

"That's so tragic!" Coral burst out. "It's like something out of a fairy tale!"

"But it's the absolute truth, believe me," replied Bertram.

"So your godfather is somebody on The Lost Isle! Do we know him?" asked Romaric.

"You don't, but Robin does," said Bertram, turning to the apprentice.

"It's Gerald!" gasped Robin, still moved by Bertram's story of his father, a Renouncer like his own father.

"Correct," confirmed Bertram, "Gerald, Master Sorcerer of the Guild! Gerald was an apprentice when my father was a squire. He was very unhappy when my father left and always tried to keep in contact, despite the distance between the Worlds. Luckily for me . . . he has been like a father to me. He's really somebody very special. I owe him so much."

"And that's how you came to be an apprentice in the Guild. . . ." went on Robin.

"That's also how I became a sorcerer, without really deserv-ing it. Or rather, without having a particular gift for magic, despite my bragging!"

A silence greeted Bertram's speech. Then, in a solemn voice, Robin responded:

"There's always a reason for everything in the end! Thank you for being so honest, Bertram. I am proud to have you as a friend."

"So am I," said Romaric, shaking Bertram's hand warmly. "And thanks for getting us out of that mess on the moor!"

"Yes, you were wonderful," agreed Coral, kissing him on the cheek.

"And now we know why you're so weird," teased Godfrey. "From now on, we'll wait to find out whether you're joking or not before we hit you!"

"What are you going to do with your gun?" asked Amber suddenly.

"I'm going to throw it into the sea from the top of the cliffs," announced Bertram without a second's hesitation. "The Lost Isle has become my only country, and I must obey its laws. Even if it is tempting to own something the Korrigans seem to fear so much!"

"I think it's for the best," said Agatha hastily, darting a worried look at Amber, who had her eye on Bertram's bag. She had had enough of Amber's reckless behavior for one day.

36

A SUMMONS

Amber and Coral had returned to Krakal, Godfrey had dropped in to see his parents in Grum before going back to the Tantreval Academy of Music, Agatha had gone home to Dashtikazar, Romaric had headed straight back to Bromotul, and Bertram to Gifdu monastery.

They had all promised not to breathe a word of their adventure to anybody, and had even sworn on Robin's apprentice's notebook, the most sacred thing they had at hand. Robin had gone back home to Penmarch, and had spent the rest of the day wandering about in a daze. His mother, totally unaware of her son's experience on the moor, had teased him relentlessly about young people overdoing the partying. He retreated to his room as soon as dinner was over.

The next day, he still felt tired when he woke up. He ran a nice hot bath and lay there thinking about the incredible adventure he had just had in the kingdom of the Korrigans.

Despite the little creatures' dirty tricks, Robin couldn't bring himself to hate them. The Korrigans' way of thinking and acting was too different from their own for them to be judged by human values. He would, however, love to find out more about the mysterious magic of the Oghams.

As for this mysterious person that Kor Mehtar wanted to hand him over to . . . "*He who has more power than a king, has a claim on you and I can't do a thing,*" he had said. Could it be The Shadow?

Then, as he dried himself and put on clean clothes, Robin thought about Amber and wondered whether she really had been bewitched. Admittedly, he hadn't actually seen Amber in a trance, but his friend's behavior was certainly very odd. Could there be a connection with the strange dreams she'd described to him?

He shook his head — he was stumped for an answer. He came out of the bathroom and decided to give his brain a rest and relax with a good book. . . .

≈ ✳ ≈ ✳ ≈

He was on the last chapter of one of his favorites, *The Three Musketeers*, which he was reading for the third time, when he felt something strange going on in his head. At first he thought he was giddy, probably due to lack of sleep over the last few nights. But the dizzy sensation grew more distinct, and Robin recognized the same signs as when his Master had spoken to him inside his head before.

He sighed with relief. Since their return from the moor, he had received no word from Quadehar, and that worried him. He tried to breathe calmly and concentrate his mind.

"Master? Master, is that you?"

He heard a distant sigh. A hoarse croak.

"Master?"

Robin began to feel worried and was wondering what he ought to do, when a voice he would have recognized anywhere echoed inside his head.

"Robin . . . listen. I don't have much time."

"Lo . . . Lord Sha!"

"That's right. I can't speak for long. I absolutely have to see you. . . ."

Robin felt a surge of panic.

Lord Sha went on, "You must trust me. Follow my instructions to the letter and everything will be fine. Now listen: Take The Door into The Real World and meet me this afternoon in a shop called Treasures of the Worlds. Most importantly, don't tell a soul. Not a soul . . ."

The voice faded before Robin could ask any questions. His heart was thumping as if it would burst. Now, Lord Sha, having pursued him through the underground passages of Gifdu, was summoning him telepathically to The Real World. . . . It was utterly crazy! He shook his head several times to make sure he hadn't been dreaming.

The most basic precaution would have been to inform the Guild at once and place himself under its protection. But, in Robin's eyes, the sorcerers' authority had diminished considerably recently, just like their concept of justice. . . . When they'd encountered one another at Gifdu, Lord Sha had not tried to harm him. Robin didn't hesitate: He would take the risk of going to meet Sha alone.

Deep down, he fervently hoped that the man in red, whom he could not bring himself to hate, even though he had stolen the *Book of the Stars* from the Guild, would provide him with some of the answers he was desperately seeking.

In case this was a trap, he scribbled a quick note to his master, which he slipped under his pillow.

He told his mother he was going for a walk, then set off in the direction of Dashtikazar and the hill beyond, where The Doors to the Two Worlds stood.

≈ ✳ ≈ ✳ ≈

The Doors to the Two Worlds looked like ordinary doors, only they were much bigger. One led to The Uncertain World, and the other to The Real World.

These two Doors, oak panels carved with numerous Graphems, were one-way only, to protect The Lost Isle from the other Worlds. But in an emergency, it was possible to use them in both directions.

The criminals of The Lost Isle were sent into permanent exile in The Uncertain World, where they became Wanderers, while the sorcerers and pursuer knights who went there on missions were able to return to The Lost Isle. However, the people of The Lost Isle who wished to live in The Real World, as Bertram's father had done, and perhaps Robin's, too, became Renouncers forever. And once, as we know, a Master Sorcerer had found a way of bringing over his orphaned godson.

Of course, to travel from one World to another you needed to know the spells to open The Doors, and above all how to use them! Only the sorcerers could do that, and even then, not all of them; for the mechanism that made it possible to travel between Worlds required a phenomenal inner energy. Robin had only managed it once and then with difficulty, and had dragged his friends with him into The Uncertain World. And now he hoped to enter The Real World with more success.

Only two Knights of the Wind were guarding The Doors this time. Now that everyone knew that The Shadow possessed the Desert Galdr and was able to come and go between The Uncertain World and The Lost Isle as he pleased, without using The Doors, tight security on the hill was deemed pointless.

Robin knew how to get past the sentries. He even felt a sense of déjà vu about the whole adventure! He called Dagaz, the Hourglass, which shaped time, and murmured it into the breeze. Without their knowledge, the knights would be affected by the Graphem and their movements would gradually slow down until they froze in midair. Time would pass much more slowly for the two men than for Robin, who slipped past them as if he were invisible, and made for The Door leading to The Real World without the slightest hindrance.

He identified the carved signs, which located his precise destination in space, and touched them with his right hand. Then he concentrated his mind and wove the Galdr that would open the door and send him far away to another world — Perthro, the Guide, so as not to miss the main Door to The Real World; Raidhu, the Chariot; Eiwaz, the Axe. He was not trembling, as he had been last time. . . . *He was becoming a real sorcerer now!* he thought to himself. Finally, when he was ready, he whispered his spell:

"*By the power of the Dice Cup and the Matrix, of the Way, of Nerthus, Ullr, and the Double Branch, Perthro above, Raidhu below, and Eiwaz in front, take me! PRE!*"

The Door to The Real World glowed briefly and Robin vanished into the void.

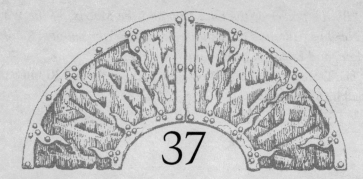

37

TREASURES OF THE WORLDS

A few seconds after he had finished chanting his spell, Robin emerged in an unknown and totally different place from the hillside he had just left. He was on the ground floor of an old building whose stones had been worn smooth by time. The doors and windows were blocked by scaffolding. Outside he could see greenery. Was it a forest? He attempted to slip out unnoticed.

"Hey you!" called a man dressed in a blue uniform with a helmet. "You're not allowed to play on the scaffolding! Can't you read?"

The man came over to help Robin out from the structure of platforms and metal poles.

"I'm sorry, Sir," apologized Robin, looking curiously about him.

The old building was in a park, in the center of a square. It looked medieval, which explained the scaffolding. It was obviously being restored.

"Don't hang around here! And be more careful," said the man in a kinder tone, won over by the boy's disarming smile. "It's dangerous."

"Yes, Sir," said Robin obediently.

He looked at the man again and realized he was a policeman, like the ones he had seen on television. He guessed that the police were roughly the equivalent of the Knights of The Lost Isle, whose job was to ensure the inhabitants' safety.

"You've got a strange accent, lad. You're not from these parts, are you?"

"Yes, I am, Sir. Well, more or less . . . It's a northern accent," stuttered Robin taking a wild guess. "Tell me, Sir, do you know a place around here called Treasures of the Worlds?"

The policeman didn't need to think for long.

"Yes, there's a shop of that name, over there, on a street in that direction . . ." he said, pointing.

"Thank you," replied Robin, setting off with a wave.

Once in the street, he stood there open-mouthed. So these were cars! He'd seen them on TV, of course, but he hadn't imagined they could be so noisy, or smell so disgusting!

Instinctively, he covered his ears and wrinkled his nose. Then he decided he'd better not draw attention to himself, and resumed a normal expression.

He was pleased to note that, as he had gathered from TV, the clothes fashions of The Real World and those of The Lost Isle were similar. So with his jeans, sweater, and canvas shoes, he did not look out of place. Even his apprentice's bag looked like a school bag.

He set off in the direction indicated by the policeman.

He wandered through the streets, looking all about him with curiosity.

Everything fascinated him. It was all so much more real than on television! The asphalt, which they had instead of cobbles, smelled so strong; the people who walked past him without saying hello seemed so unfriendly; the dull roar of the cars which drove at top speed between the buildings was so alien to him . . .

He asked for directions several times from passersby who were kind enough to stop, and eventually found the shop he was looking for.

On a grimy window was written TREASURES OF THE WORLDS, ANTIQUES in faded lettering.

A tattered canvas awning hung down over the front, making it impossible to see inside.

Robin hesitated, then pushed open the door. It creaked horribly and set off a shrill bell. The boy closed the door behind him and stepped into the dimly lit room. Everything seemed to have been designed to put off potential customers!

There was light filtering through a curtain at the back of the shop. He went over to it, hesitated, then drew back the heavy fabric.

"Come in, Robin. I was expecting you."

Sitting cross-legged on a carpet, wrapped in his vast bloodred cloak, Lord Sha beckoned him into the room.

Robin looked about him. The shelves were laden with treasures of all sorts. He was surprised to recognize objects that he had already come across in The Uncertain World.

He was delighted to see, placed on a cushion at the right

height, a Gambouri, a flower of the sands, which Kyle and his people gathered in the Ravenous Desert and sold in Ferghana. But he curbed his curiosity and sat down on the carpet facing Lord Sha.

"I knew you'd come," began Sha. "You weren't really afraid of me the other day, in the corridors of Gifdu. And then, for an apprentice who destroyed Thunku's palace with barely more than a sneeze, crossing over into The Real World must have been easy!"

Robin stared at Lord Sha's smiling face for a moment.

"Is there anything you don't know about me?" he eventually asked.

Sha gave a little laugh.

"Oh, I'm sure there is. Do you want something to drink?"

"A hot chocolate, please. If you have any . . ."

Lord Sha nodded, picked up a saucepan and poured in some milk and cocoa powder. He stirred it and heated it up on a little stove next to the oil lamp that lit the room with its mellow glow.

"I'm very fond of The Real World," said Sha conspiratorially. "Of course, it's not as good as The Lost Isle, but it is quieter than The Uncertain World. I spend half my time here!"

"And what do you do in The Real World?" asked Robin, gratefully taking the mug of hot chocolate that Sha placed in front of him.

"Officially I'm an antiques dealer, specializing in rare and exotic objects! That explains my long absences. Unofficially . . . it's a secret!"

"You sell objects that you bring back from The Uncertain World?" asked Robin in surprise.

"Correct," admitted Lord Sha with a smile.

"Thanks to the Desert Galdr? Is that how you do it?"

"No. The Desert Galdr only works between The Lost Isle and The Uncertain World. To come and go from The Real World without being noticed, I use Doors that I built myself."

He paused, seeing Robin's startled expression, then he went on, "I don't think you understand. Perhaps you're not aware that the Graphems have no power in The Real World?"

"No power? You mean . . . If I'm attacked and I call Thursaz, nothing will happen?" asked Robin anxiously.

"Nothing at all. At best, you'll only frighten away your attacker by screaming!"

"That's not funny!"

"Sorry," apologized Sha. "I was trying to . . ."

"I was asking about the Graphems, which don't work in The Real World!" Robin insisted.

"You're right, it's not funny," agreed Sha, picking up a teapot and pouring himself a cup of hot tea. "Whereas on The Lost Isle magic makes us powerful and commands respect, here, we feel disagreeably ordinary."

"If the power of Graphems doesn't reach here," queried Robin, "how did you manage to contact me?"

"When I contacted you, I was in The Uncertain World. The Graphems work there, as long as you remember to adapt them. I used one of The Doors to The Lost Isle to establish communication. On the other hand, as I was saying to you, the absence of magic in The Real World means you have to use Doors to come and go. I have one here, in my shop, and another in my tower, at Jaghatel. Actually, that's why it took me so long to contact you after our last encounter. The Door I'd built at Jaghatel had been damaged and I had to repair it. . . ."

Robin became flustered and took a deep breath.

"Look, I absolutely have to know the truth. Quadehar, my master, is in a lot of trouble at the moment and it's very important . . ."

"What do you want to know?" asked Sha in a friendly tone.

"Was it you who . . . was it you who killed the sorcerers at the Tower of Jaghatel?"

Lord Sha's amethyst eyes met Robin's directly.

"I'm going to be honest with you, and everything I tell you will be the truth. You have my word."

38

SECRETS

Robin sensed that the man was sincere. Lord Sha settled himself more comfortably on the big carpet covering the floor of the room at the back of the shop and continued:

"I had absolutely nothing to do with the ambush of the sorcerers at Jaghatel. The day before the attack, my steward had given me an anonymous message telling me that you would be at Gifdu, in the company of the lesser sorcerers. In the past, my mysterious correspondent had given me accurate information; I had no reason not to believe him this time. There you were, almost alone, at Gifdu, it was now or never . . . When I got back to Jaghatel, I found the bodies of the sorcerers, and of the Orks who were under the order of Thunku. I also found my tower had been ransacked. . . ."

"And yet," objected Robin, dubiously, "Commander Thunku is your friend, isn't he? And he did send Gommons and Orks on your orders to The Lost Isle, to kidnap me, didn't he?"

Lord Sha looked thunderstruck.

"Thunku is my friend, it's true, but he is also the friend of all sorts of scum! To be more exact, Thunku is the friend of those who pay him or of those he's afraid of. As for what you're accusing me of . . . in the name of the gods, no! I never tried to have you kidnapped!"

Robin could see that Lord Sha was telling the truth.

"Who else, if not you, then, would have been capable of sending Orks to The Lost Isle?"

Sha thought for a moment.

"Several names spring to mind, but one is enough: The Shadow."

"Do you know who The Shadow is?"

"Nobody knows."

"At least," admitted Robin with relief, "it's not you!"

The man laughed.

"Me, The Shadow? How ridiculous! Who could think such a thing?"

"The sorcerers who attacked your tower," replied Robin quietly.

The smile vanished from Sha's face.

"But that's plain ridiculous."

Then Robin told him about Godfrey's last adventure at Jaghatel, climbing the tower and seeing a mysterious figure.

". . . and so the Guild concluded that you could be The Shadow," ended Robin.

"I understand more clearly now," Sha sighed. "Listen carefully. My real name is Yorwan. I was born on The Lost Isle. Just like you, I was an apprentice of the Guild, and I was even made a sorcerer. One day, and it was truly against my will, you must believe me, I had to leave The Lost Isle in a hurry to take a precious book of spells, the *Book of the Stars*, which you have no doubt heard of, to a safe hiding place. . . ."

"Yes. Master Quadehar told me your story. But he told me that you'd stolen the book. That's what everyone on The Lost Isle believes."

Sha sighed heavily again.

"I know that's what they believe . . . and what does it matter? The main thing is that the *Book of the Stars* has been kept safely hidden all these years. . . . But something terrible has happened, and that is why I have asked you to meet me here. When I looked inside your mind, at Gifdu, I immediately saw that you were somebody who could be relied on in a crisis. And I need you. I need you to convince your master to help me. In the past, Master Quadehar was my closest friend. . . . Now listen carefully. You must tell him that the *Book of the Stars*, which was until now in my possession, has disappeared, and this time for good. Somebody stole it from my tower while I was looking for you at Gifdu. . . ."

"But Master Quadehar already thinks you're a thief! He'll never believe me. . . ." Robin shook his head.

Sha's face clouded over.

"That's why I need your help, Robin. The other day, I made a mistake, the first for years: In my joy at finding you, I left behind the book that I was responsible for and which I'd never let out of my sight until that moment."

Robin was trembling.

"You said, at Gifdu, that you had mistaken me for someone else. . . ."

Sha gazed at the boy, who had turned very pale.

"Do you really want to know?"

"Yes, I want to know!"

"About fourteen years ago, when I was a young sorcerer, I fell madly in love with a wonderful young woman I'd met during the Samain festival. She shared my feelings, and we were betrothed. We were about to get married when suddenly I was forced to leave with the *Book of the Stars*. Don't ask me why, I can't tell you. Only that it was vital for The Lost Isle . . . so I left without having had the time to explain my actions to the woman I loved. I was crazy with grief. Many years later, I received a mysterious letter, written in the same hand as the recent one informing me of your presence at Gifdu. This letter informed me that my beloved, whom I'd left behind on The Lost Isle, had borne a child by me. . . . A child that the *Book of the Stars* had deprived me of, for I had chosen duty over love!"

Sha was emotional, and his voice shook slightly. When he finished:

"That woman's name was Alicia. Alicia Penmarch."

Robin's heart stood still. He stammered, "But then . . . so you're . . . you're . . ."

"I should be your father, Robin. But I saw the truth inside you. I'm sorry, Robin, but you're not my son. My informer was lying."

Robin was speechless with emotion.

Nothing made any sense. . . .

He asked again, "Why . . . why did you wait so long before trying to find me?"

"I only learned of your existence after many years, remember. And besides, when I had to leave your mother, Urian, her brother, went into a wild rage. He couldn't know that I had to leave The Lost Isle for an important reason. And, if it had been up to me alone, I would have stayed with Alicia forever. The hatred of your uncle, who could rely on the support of the Brotherhood, and perhaps also the fear of seeing your mother again after all these years, prevented me from coming to find you on The Lost Isle. Your presence at Gifdu, far from the knights and in the absence of the powerful sorcerers who could have protected you, was the first real opportunity I had to make contact with you. . . ."

But Robin was no longer listening. He was racked by a terrible doubt.

39

A WOMAN WITH
GREEN EYES

Robin could barely hold back his tears as he bid farewell to Lord Sha. The man in the red cloak was deeply affected and tried to comfort him, assuring him that surely, one day the truth would be revealed.

He did not know what to reply when Robin asked him if he knew the Renouncer who could be his father. Lord Sha was not in touch with Renouncers. To cheer him up, Lord Sha invited Robin to help himself to anything he liked from the shop, but Robin wanted nothing, not even the desert flower that reminded him of Kyle, his faraway friend.

Robin left the antiques shop but did not linger in The Real World. Everything was too fast, and too noisy. The cars, the people rushing along the pavements without giving him a second glance, all made him feel uncomfortable, but above all, he had something important to do on The Lost Isle.

Lord Sha had explained to him that The Door in his shop was programmed to give access only to The Uncertain World. So to return to The Lost Isle, he had to go back the same way he had come. He waited until he was alone in the square and then he slipped inside the medieval building.

On one of the walls, hidden among the stonecutters' signs, Robin could make out the Graphems that would get him home. As if he had been doing it all his life, he automatically wove his Galdr and, after a brief whirling through the void which was beginning to feel familiar, he found himself back on The Lost Isle, in front of The Door to The Real World.

The two knights he had put under a spell upon leaving were still asleep, so Robin took advantage and made a quick getaway from the hillside.

≋ ✳ ≋ ✳ ≋

He reached the dolmen just outside Dashtikazar where he had so often met Master Quadehar. The same dolmen beside which his master had disclosed the mysteries and revealed the beauty of the *Book of the Stars*.

He clambered onto the stone slab and sat down cross-legged.

He had to get to his master as soon as possible, and tell him what he'd found out about the theft and the recent disappearance of the *Book of the Stars*. He had given his word to Lord Sha. But to do that, he would have to use the Lokk for mental communication. It was the first time he had tried it. He set about mixing Berkana, the Graphem of the Silver Birch and the Ear, used for communication between the spirits, Elhaz, which opened locks, and Isaz, which assisted concentration.

Having constructed the spell, he focused on Quadehar as hard as he could and projected his Lokk, which vanished into space. Robin was unsure. Had he gotten it right? He decided to try with somebody else. He conjured up Bertram's face in his mind and sent the Lokk energetically in his direction. Soon, he heard the young sorcerer's voice inside his head.

"Don't shout so loudly! Who's calling me?"

"It's me, Robin. Sorry. It's the first time I've used this Lokk!"

"Robin!" cried his friend. "I'm so happy to hear you! Can I help you? Are you in trouble?"

"Perhaps . . . I'm trying to contact Master Quadehar, and I can't reach him."

"That's not surprising. Gerald has just told me that Quadehar has left The Lost Isle for The Uncertain World, with your Uncle Urian and another knight called Valentino!"

Robin was devastated.

"That's disastrous. . . . I've got something very, very important to tell him . . ."

"Very important? Very, very important?" parroted Bertram.

"Very, very important. Crucial, even!"

"And . . . what might that be?"

"Please, Bertram, don't tease me. I can't tell you anything! It's for Master Quadehar's ears only."

"Well, why don't you go and meet him in The Uncertain World?" replied Bertram, peeved.

Robin paused. "That's what I'll do, you're right. . . ."

"Hey, Robin! I was only joking, you know me!"

"Well, I'm not joking, Bertram. What I have to tell Quadehar is of the utmost importance. . . ."

"In that case . . . in that case . . . I'm coming with you!"

The apprentice hesitated for a moment. It was out of the question to drag his friends into another dangerous adventure! But Bertram? Deep down, he felt better at the thought of having him by his side.

Bertram insisted, "Well, Robin? We're on, right?"

"OK. Meet you tomorrow at noon at my place."

"Good, good, very good! So I'm off to get ready. See you tomorrow!"

"Tomorrow."

The communication broke off. Despite the turmoil he felt as a result of Lord Sha's confession, Robin couldn't help smiling at the thought of Bertram's enthusiasm. He was a strange boy, but so . . . well . . . so good!

He jumped off the dolmen and headed for Penmarch. There was another important thing he had to do. More important even than the highly important revelations he had to make to the most important sorcerer of all. . .

〰 ✳ 〰 ✳ 〰

Robin arrived home just as his mother was setting the table for dinner.

"Perfect timing!" she called out. "Wash your hands and finish setting the table while I take the roast out of the oven."

Robin raced over to the sink and rinsed his hands.

"With soap!" commanded his mother, who had her back to him.

He sighed and asked himself how she could see what he was

up to without looking at him. That was even beyond the skill of this young apprentice sorcerer!

He did as he was told, and set out the glasses, knives, and forks on the table. Then he sat down. Alicia placed the steaming dish in front of him.

"Mmm! That smells good! What are we having with it?"

"Mashed potatoes!"

"Yum, Mom. I love you!"

"Go on, eat it while it's hot."

Robin sliced the roast and served his mother and then himself.

He was trembling slightly. He had promised himself that he would ask her something that evening, something that he had never dared ask before. He had to know. He wanted to smother the doubt that was tormenting him once and for all.

He looked at her and thought she looked very beautiful in the lamp light. He felt a surge of love for her. No, he couldn't spoil the atmosphere. And yet . . .

"Mom . . ." he began in a strained voice.

"Yes, darling?" replied Alicia, frowning at the sight of his worried face. "What's wrong?"

"I wanted . . . I wanted to ask you something. . . ."

Robin would never have believed that it could be so hard.

"I wanted to know whether you had had another husband apart from Dad."

There. He'd said it. And now he wished he hadn't. He didn't dare look at his mother. Alicia stared at him for a long time, then she rose, walked over to him, and put her arms around him. Robin hugged her back.

"My darling, my poor darling. I know how difficult it is for you! I know, believe me, I know! But listen carefully: There has never been any man in my life other than your father. And it doesn't matter what he did, or that his courage failed him. I believe that, even today, I wouldn't be able to help loving him."

Robin sobbed quietly. All the pressure that had weighed on his shoulders for such a long time was released with his tears.

"There, there, darling," his mother soothed, cuddling him. "I feel as if I'm holding my pretty baby again!"

"Your . . . pretty . . . baby?" asked Robin still shaken by sobs, wiping his eyes.

"My beautiful baby. So beautiful that a nurse at Dashtikazar hospital, where you were born, even tried to kidnap you! I remember as if it were yesterday. She was very beautiful with long fair hair and green eyes. . . . "

Robin thought his heart would stop beating a second time. A woman with green eyes . . . like in Amber's dreams! A woman who had tried to kidnap him . . .

"Don't worry, darling," Alicia quickly added when she saw Robin's shocked look. "She didn't get far. Look, since you're here with me! The nurse was found soon afterward, wandering through the corridors. She handed you back without protest. She was dismissed, and I don't know what became of her."

"And . . . are you sure it was definitely me?" Robin panicked. "I mean, the baby that the woman gave back to you?"

"Of course, my darling!" exclaimed Alicia. "You had your identity bracelet with your name on it! And even though all babies look alike, I would have picked you out among a thousand babies. Who else would you be?"

"I don't know, and that's the problem," murmured Robin, too softly for his mother to hear.

Thirteen years of certainties had just collapsed like a house of cards.

40

SEEING STARS

Even though he was exhausted, Robin was unable to get to sleep. His thoughts were banging around in his head and it felt like it was going to burst.

When Alicia came in to kiss him good night with infinite tenderness, he pretended to be asleep. She murmured soothing words of love, and stroked his hair for a long time. Robin wished that moment could last forever. He wanted to forget everything, escape from his tormented thoughts. But during the night, he woke up plagued with doubts again. His heart began to pound, his fists clenched and unclenched repeatedly, and his eyes remained wide open in the darkness of his room.

After a while, he decided to get up. Once on his feet, he felt better. Dressed in his light blue pajamas, he went over to the window and drew the curtains. Outside, high in the sky, the stars twinkled, and there was a luminous halo around the moon. Robin opened the window and filled his lungs with the cool night air. He shivered. His eyes sought out the constellations. He didn't know whether he should love or hate these stars that had turned his life upside down and which led him down terrifying paths. He felt smaller and more alone than ever under the immense canopy of the sky.

As if to comfort Robin, the image of Quadehar's smiling face came into his mind. He immediately felt calmer. Perhaps it was stupid, but he was deeply convinced that nothing serious could happen to him as long as Master Quadehar kept watch over him.

He stood for a while longer gazing at the stars before going back to bed where, overcome with tiredness, he fell asleep.

≋ ✳ ≋ ✳ ≋

A fire of dry twigs crackled and cast its flickering light onto the section of crumbling wall that was sheltering Urian, Valentino, and Quadehar from the howling wind. The three men had set up camp in a desolate moorland spot, somewhere between Virdu and The Infested Sea. The investigation they had been carrying out for several days now in The Uncertain World, as they sought precise information on the Jaghatel ambush, had proved disappointing so far. But it was too soon to lose heart. In silence, they had dined on bread, dried goat's meat, and ewe's milk cheese, then they had settled down for the night.

Urian, enveloped in a thick bearskin, was already asleep. His snores made Valentino smile as he said to Quadehar, "I haven't had to put up with that racket for a long time!"

"Come, Valentino, stop complaining. I'm sure you've missed it."

"You're right. Good Lord, I feel alive again! The smell of a nearby fire is intoxicating! What about you, Sorcerer, what do you miss?"

Quadehar did not reply straight away. He allowed his gaze to roam among the stars that were so different, yet so similar to those of The Lost Isle.

"Oddly enough, Valentino," he eventually replied, "it's not something, but somebody that I miss. A little boy who must be feeling very alone as he faces up to his destiny, back there on The Lost Isle."

"You mean Robin?"

"Yes."

"You've grown very fond of the boy, haven't you?"

"To be honest, I have only one fear, and that is that one day I might lose him."

"And yet you've left him alone. . . ."

"He's with his friends and under the protection of a young sorcerer . . . but above all, I have faith in him. Robin is a highly resourceful apprentice."

Valentino hesitated, then decided not to pursue the conversation. He yawned, lay down under his woollen blanket, and allowed the gentle crackling of the flames to lull him to sleep.

But Quadehar sat there for a long time, his gaze lost in the vast starry heavens.

END OF PART TWO

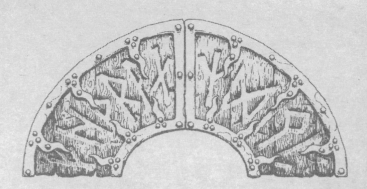

ROBIN'S NOTEBOOK

THE GRAPHEM ALPHABET

The Graphems are the 24 letters of a magic alphabet, based on the stars, which make it possible to enter the Wyrd. They are like keys that unlock and reveal the secrets inside.

A Graphem is defined by its number (order and position within the group), its shape (name and appearance), and its content (symbolic associations, other names, and powers).

Each Graphem has several powers. When Graphems are mentally summoned (visualized) and then projected (shouted or whispered), they have a simple and direct effect.

MUDRA

These are movements of the hand in the air which reproduce the shapes of the Graphems to invoke them (similar to the Stadha, the postures that mimic the Graphems). Mudra are quick and discreet. But watch out: The Graphems used in a Mudra are less powerful than those called out or invoked using the Stadha. So these magic movements should only be used when there's no other option: in a difficult situation which requires discretion, like in a Korrigans' cave, for example!

FEHU (f)

URUZ (u/v)

THURSAZ (t)

ELHAZ (z)

INGWAZ (ng/gn)

THE LOKK

The Lokk is a spell where you mix the Graphems. It's different from the Galdr. In the Galdr, the Graphems are words that make up a sentence, whereas in the Lokk, the Graphems are the letters that make up a word. The Galdr weaves together and links, the Lokk dissolves and mixes. The Galdr is easier to form, but is less powerful than the Lokk; the Lokk is stronger but more complicated to construct than the Galdr. So, if in doubt, or in an emergency, it's better to rely on a Galdr than a Lokk!

Example: The Communication Lokk, based on Berkana, the Graphem that enables you to communicate with the spirits. It also uses Elhaz, which clears paths, and Isaz, which aids concentration. So I place Berkana at the center of my mind, then I send it to sleep. Then I call up Elhaz and Isaz, which I also send to sleep. Then I pile them on top of each other, and heat them until they're red hot and melt into a single new Graphem, Beteleir. Then I awaken this new Graphem and I send it by projecting the face of the person I want to contact onto it. Once this person has been found, communication is established by concentrating hard, and takes place silently, inside our heads (the Lokk ensures the exchange of thoughts between the two minds). There's no need for any magic words but, if you want to make a Lokk more flexible and more docile, it is also possible to tame it (then you emphasize the Graphem at the center of the Lokk, in this case Berkana): "You, the Silver Birch, you the Ear, you who now make one with the Brilliant and the Swan, as the blind need guidance, crackle and burn beyond space and the word, lead me to the spirit I wish to communicate with! BETELEIR!"

BETELEIR

$$\text{B} + \text{Y} + | = \text{B}$$

Two protective spells, the Armor of Elhaz and the Helmet of Terror:

For protection against a major physical or magic attack against which both Thursaz and Naudhiz (Graphems for warding off attacks) are ineffective, there are two powerful spells: a Galdr, the Armor of Elhaz, and a Lokk, the Helmet of Terror, both built around the Graphem Elhaz.

The Armor of Elhaz Galdr is woven by combining six Elhaz (in your head, in the air, or on the ground), using the following magic words: *"By the power of Erda and Kari, Rind, Hir, and Loge, Elhaz in front, Elhaz behind, Elhaz to the left, Elhaz to the right, Elhaz above, and Elhaz below, Elhaz protect me! ALU!"* (basic magic word which generally reinforces Graphems used on their own).

The Helmet of Terror Lokk is created by mixing Elhaz eight times, in the air above your head or on the ground beneath your feet. The eight fused Elhaz form a new Graphem, an eight-pointed star, each point ending in a trident: Egishjamur. But if just one of the eight Elhaz isn't drawn properly, that's enough to invalidate the Lokk. Whereas if one of the six Elhaz for the Armor is badly drawn, the Galdr will still function although it may be a bit weak. That's why you've got to know what you're doing before attempting a Lokk, whereas a Galdr will do the same job, even if it is not as powerful!

And here's an improvement: to hold back Lord Sha in the underground tunnels of Gifdu, I used the Helmet of Terror and the Armor of Elhaz together! First of all I created the Helmet of Terror Lokk and I wove the Armor Galdr using Egishjamur instead of Elhaz, like a normal Graphem! Master Quadehar told me that I wasn't the first person to have thought of it, but I was the only one to have accomplished it successfully! Thanks to my very powerful Ond. . . .

EGISHJAMUR

THE KORRIGAN OGHAMS

The Korrigans, little creatures of the moors, possess a different magic from ours. Little is known about it, and I couldn't even find much in the libraries at Gifdu. This is a summary of what I found out in Kor Mehtar's palace.

Korrigan magic is older than that of the sorcerers. It draws its strength not from the stars, but from the earth and the moon. It also uses an alphabet: the Ogham alphabet. Oghams are always red as a reminder of the blood ties that link the earth to the moon. The Oghams have the names of plants (plants grow in the earth — the interior, under the moonlight — the exterior). The spells are chanted in Korrigani, accompanied by dances. It seems to call upon the individual Oghams (there is no equivalent of our Galdr).

Apparently, long ago, before the arrival of *The Book of the Stars* on The Lost Isle, we, too, used to practice Ogham magic.

THE GRAPHEM ALPHABET
KENAZ

Position: Sixth Graphem
Other names: the Craftsman, the Torch
Associations: fire, which warms and devors
Powers: stimulates creativity, the brain; awakens; can destroy "sorrow makes man pale"

BE CAREFUL!
USE WITH CAUTION

GEBU

Position: Seventh Graphem
Other names: Sharp, Gefj
Associations: gifts, trade, sacrifice
Powers: establishes communication; protects emotional relationships and trade ("the haven of the dispossessed"); stimulates the circulation of energy between the sky, humans, and the earth

YERA

Position: Twelfth Graphem
Other names: The Reject, Frodi, the Warm season
Associations: the cycle, harmony (between heaven and earth)
Powers: speeds up or slows down the effects of magic spells; frees, purifies; helps acquire goods

BERKANA

Position: Eighteenth Graphem
Other names: the Silver Birch, Hel, the Ear
Associations: inner balance, the Graphem of that which is hidden, protected, internalized (depth)
Powers: vehicle; allows communication between the spirits; helps fulfill plans

LAUKAZ

Position: Twenty-first Graphem
Other names: the Hook, the Foot
Associations: primal water (the ocean); the fluid life force (the water equivalent of Uruz); the seed, the non-manifest ("all precious stones are gold")
Powers: talisman (long-term protection); powerful aid to all growth processes; liquefies, removes obstacles; medicinal Graphem (fights infections)